CRANNÓG 44 spring 2017

Editorial Board

Sandra Bunting
Ger Burke
Jarlath Fahy
Tony O'Dwyer

ISSN 1649-4865
ISBN 978-1-907017-46-9

Cover image: 'Worn By Sanctity ... Ambulatory at High Island'
by Margaret Irwin
Cover image sourced by Sandra Bunting
Cover design by Wordsonthestreet
Published by Wordsonthestreet for Crannóg magazine
www.wordsonthestreet.com   @wordsstreet

All writing copyrighted to rightful owners in accordance with The Berne Convention

Contents

Stateless
    Brian Kirk 6
Bucharest, 1989
    Shannon Kelly 7
Absences
    Máiríde Woods 8
Iscariot
    Anne Walsh Donnelly 9
Song of the Birds
    Karla Van Vliet 15
For Mr T
    Karina Tynan 16
I Have Bent My Body into the Shape of a Harp
    Liz Dolan 17
Everything After
    Jonathan Starke 18
Old Day and Birds
    Clare Sawtell 20
All for Love
    John Reinhart 21
Hunger
    Chelsea Steinauer-Scudder 22
Child Proof
    Shannon Quinn 26
At a Cinema Near You
    Gary Allen 27
The Dark is Never a Murmur
    Simon Anton Diego Baena 28
Trouble Crossing the Bridge
    Diana Powell 29
This Terrain
    Christine Pacyk 36
The Carrington Chimney
    Mark O'Flynn 37
Southern Skies
    Mark Mullee 38
Mole
    Elizabeth Morton 39
Until the Call Comes
    Geraldine Mills 40
I Want You More Than Peace or Quiet Sleep
    Lisa Morris 45

Corps de Ballet
   James Martyn Joyce 46
Taking off the Mask
   Brenda Donoghue 47
Your Bicycle
   Joe Carrick-Varty 52
Grease Proofing
   Emily Cullen 53
Three Strong Words
   Kate Dempsey 54
Irish Mammies, Beware
   Kate Ennals 55
The Ballad of Cross-Eyed Kate
   Jarlath Fahy 60
There Are Only a Few Things
   Mary Melvin Geoghegan 61
I Imagine You at Your Secrétaire
   Anton Floyd 62
Plum Marker
   Shauna Gilligan 63
Prostitute
   Agnieszka Filipek 68
Life is Not a Dancer
   Barbara De Franceschi 69
Thief
   Honor Duff 70
Night Vigil on the N7
   Ríona Judge McCormack 71
Off the Record
   Maurice Devitt 76
Morning Mass in Galway
   Michael Farry 77
Somewhere North of the Plaza Hotel
   Paddy Kehoe 78
Bog
   Rozz Lewis 79
Summer Is Colt Fast
   Gerry Stewart 84
Sounds
   Wei Huan (Translated by Liang Yujing) 85
Violet
   Eoin O'Neill 86
Artist's Statement
   Margaret Irwin 90
Biographical Details 91

The Galway Study Centre

Since 1983, the Galway Study Centre has been dedicating itself to giving an excellent education service to post-primary school students in Galway.

info@galwaystudycentre.ie
Tel: 091-564254

www.galwaystudycentre.ie

BRIDGE MILLS
GALWAY LANGUAGE CENTRE
Established 1987

Small family run language school
ACELS and MEI RELSA approved
Courses in English, Italian, Polish, Portuguese, Spanish, German and Japanese
Teacher training including CELT TEFL

Telephone: +353 (0) 91 566 468 Fax: +353 (0) 91 564 122
Email: info@galwaylanguage.com

Submissions for Crannóg 45 open March 1st until March 31st
Publication date is June 30th 2017

Crannóg is published three times a year in spring, summer and autumn.

Submission Times: Month of November for spring issue. Month of March for summer issue. Month of July for autumn issue.

We will <u>not read</u> submissions sent outside these times.

POETRY: *Send no more than three poems. Each poem should be under 50 lines.*

PROSE: *Send one story. Stories should be under 2,000 words.*

We do not accept postal submissions.

When emailing your submission we require **three** *things:*

1. *The text of your submission included both in body of email and as a Word attachment (this is to ensure correct layout. We may, however, change your layout to suit our publication).*
2. *A brief bio in the third person. Include this both in body and in attachment.*
3. *A postal address for contributor's copy in the event of publication.*

To learn more about Crannóg Magazine, or purchase copies of the current issue, log on to our website:

www.crannogmagazine.com

STATELESS　　　　　　　　　　　　　　　　　　　BRIAN KIRK

It's no holiday camp here believe me,
no one smiles or sings, there are no games
beyond the extended waiting for your name
to be called. Kids sleep under lock and key,
dreaming a life where they are nobody.
Days are a joyless grind, always the same,
confined within the rules that we disclaim.
We holiday in camps abroad beside the sea,
equate our leisure with our right to be,
we swim in spotless pools and dine sans shame,
our wallets fat, refusing to feel blame,
defensive. We are willing detainees,
incarcerated, yet there is no fence
to hold us, we squander independence.

BUCHAREST, 1989 — SHANNON KELLY

When all of this is over,
there will be an abundance of meat,
milk, and white sugar.

We will find a little television set,
rusted but functional,
tune the antenna,
and watch for hours, if we like.

Every neighbourhood will be our own –
and enough toilet paper to last us
through the next three winters,
the skirmishes on the street.

Our coffee we will drink with relish.
What I do not finish, I will dump
down the drain with no pang of remorse.

When all of this is over,
we will bribe an officer
to let us near that house
where the basement cinema sits empty,
and the bedrooms are broken stale replicas of Versailles.

There will be a group of bony men
in all black who stumble around,
slipping into foundational cracks,
helping themselves to the furs inside,
picking red flecks off the swimming pool mosaic.

Someone will set fire to the front lawn, someone
will savour the last hidden bottle of Maramureş wine,
crawling into a cupboard and sipping it there through wild teeth;
Someone will set the peacocks free.

ABSENCES MÁIRÍDE WOODS

The absences rise up
like sandbanks between tides,
half hidden, yet shimmering
beneath damp surfaces, meagre texts.
I hear this call of curlews, of things unbearably lost:
the debris of our lives is washed, spun, salted
exposed upon the shore; past its best,
leading to embarrassment; the things
we should have done or said
upturned like denatured evidence
for some stray beachcomber,
while the damp sand dries out
and recasts itself in whorls
around the shallow pools
once vigorous with splashing feet.

ISCARIOT

ANNE WALSH DONNELLY

He taps on the ceiling of my skull.

'Leave me alone, Iscariot.'

I close my eyes and squeeze him into the cell at the back of my head.

'You're beyond redemption,' he says.

That's what he keeps telling me but I don't want to believe him.

I hope Maisie's letter comes today. That will quieten him. I love the wintergreen smell of her envelopes, the thrill of touching paper she touched, tracing my fingers around her words. Imagining I'm the pen in her hand as she writes, the feel of her fingers on my hard, slim body. I still can't believe my luck, that she was one of the people who answered my advertisement in the *New York Times* requesting a pen pal.

'She's given up on you, can't say I blame her,' says Iscariot.

Rubbish. She's been writing every week for the last five years. Isn't she entitled to miss one or even two?

'Hah. So much for your grand plans if you ever get out of here,' says Iscariot.

'When ... not ... if.'

'Do you really think she'll want you?'

'You're the only person who really knows me,' she'd said in one of her letters.

She doesn't tell her co-workers how she dances to heavy metal music every morning before work. They'd laugh if I told them and we're too busy looking after the patients to chat, she said. They'd laugh too if she told them about her dreams of living at the foot of a mountain and waking up in the morning to the sound of a gushing stream. And even her brother doesn't know that she pretended to cry when her father died. I pretended to cry when I killed mine. Of course I haven't told her that. Yet.

'She didn't like your drawing,' says Iscariot.

'You don't know that.'

It took me weeks to get it right, though it was worth it and drawing kept Iscariot at bay. My portrait of her was tasteful, I thought. Okay, I've never actually seen her photo. She didn't have one nice enough to send me. I drew the woman I knew from her words. Her forearms covered the dark-nippled breasts I had imagined and her hands lay crossways over the apex of her fleshy thighs. Short, spikey, black hair. I couldn't picture her in long tresses.

'If she knew what we're capable of ...'

'Shut the hell up, Iscariot. There's no "we" anymore.'

'I got your picture, thanks,' she said in her next letter.

That was it. No other mention and I thought maybe I'd messed everything up. Or maybe she had a boyfriend or husband that she'd never told me about and he'd found the portrait and bashed her. That thought had me pulling grey hairs out of the beard covering my scarred jaw. But she still kept writing.

I drew a picture of her bedroom last week. She likes cotton sheets so I covered her double bed with deep-purple ones, no duvet needed. Her cream body spread across the dark sheets. I keep that picture under my pillow.

I wonder what Mother would think if she could see me drawing pictures.

'Your father would have laughed,' says Iscariot.

I think Mother would have loved to know that I'd found something within me that I didn't know I had; something beautiful. And then she'd know that she wasn't insane to love me. She never stopped till the day she died even though Iscariot took me from her a long time before her coffin was lowered into the grave.

Sometimes the people who write want to know what has me here for so long.

'Self-defence.'

That's how I frame it.

'Only losers with nothing else to do write to men like you,' says Iscariot.

I go over to the windowsill and study the plastic pieces on my chessboard. Manhattan Bob has me in 'check' and today's the deadline for me to write back and tell him my next move. Don't think I'm going to win this one. He's already taken my Rooks and a Bishop. I'll get my revenge in the next game.

I've to finish reading *The Republic* today too so I can write to Dean and tell him what I thought of it.

'*The Republic*. Hah. It's far from that you were reared,' says Iscariot.

Dean's a lecturer, teaches philosophy in a university in Boston. He's introduced me to the writings of Plato, Socrates even Descartes. I think therefore I am, that's what Descartes says.

'You think of me, too,' says Iscariot.

'So bloody what.'

'Writing, reading, drawing, playing chess. Waste of time.'

What am I supposed to do? Curl up in the corner of my cell and wait till they let me out? There's nobody to visit since Mother died.

Someone jams a key into the lock of my cell door. I spin on my heel and turn my back on the chessboard. Mike pushes open the door, casting a grey shadow on the cell's white-tiled floor. He coughs as he puts an envelope on my table.

'Just the one letter today, Bill.'

'Thanks, that cough of yours is getting worse,' I say.

He takes a tissue from his pocket and wipes his mouth.

'Yeah, that's what the wife keeps saying.'

'You should go see a doctor.'

'She says that too. Says it'll kill me yet. But it's hard to kill a bad thing, eh, Bill.?'

'I guess that's why we're both still here,' I say.

As soon as the door bangs behind him, I grab the envelope, turn it over to see if it has Maisie's navy fountain pen lettering that always leans to the left. It's a brown envelope, like the ones she uses, only bigger and the letters are straight, no softness in them at all.

Bloody post, it can be awful slow sometimes. I throw the envelope on the bed. I'll open it later. Back to my chessboard. If I move my King to the left, Bob will take my Queen. But I don't think I have any other option.

I wipe my forehead and rub a damp hand in my beard. I can feel the envelope glaring at my hunched back. Who could it be from? Don't recognise the handwriting.

'Open it,' says Iscariot.

Without further thought I move my King to the left and abandon the chessboard. The mattress springs recoil as I sit on the bed. I tear open the envelope. Out it falls. A faint flutter, then a square lands on my knees. I unfold it, recognising the anaemic-blue paper. Catch my breath. I place the drawing on my pillow and read the letter accompanying it.

Dear Mr Creighton

Aunt Maisie specifically requested that this portrait be sent back to you on her demise.

Demise? Fuck.

She had a lovely death.

Is this guy for real? Some sort of sick joke. I throw the letter on the bed and dig my knuckles into my eyes. My abdominal muscles clench. She couldn't be dead. She's too young. Maybe it's Iscariot playing with the words that my eyes are sending to my cerebral cortex. I grab the letter again.

She passed away peacefully in her sleep. The way we'd all like to go at that age.

That age? Iscariot does his Dracula laugh.

'You fool, she was only a young one in your head.'

She lived a long and happy life and loved getting your letters. It brightened her days in the care home.

Care home?

But … she lived in an apartment in Harlem. The heavy air in the summer made her want to strip naked and lie in a cold bath every evening. And I'd be there sitting on the edge, holding her towel.

You are quite an artist. Your portrait showed my aunt in a way I'd never seen her before. A bit disconcerting, perhaps. But then I don't think I ever really knew her. I don't think anyone did.

The letter helicopters to the floor. I jump off the bed and pace from window to cell door and back again.

No … No … NO!

I bang my fist on the windowsill, send the chess pieces flying. The sound of metal grinding against metal reverberates around the cell as the key turns in the lock again.

'Dinner,' says Mike.

I don't turn around. The plastic tray scrapes off my formica-topped table as he sets it down and I cover my ears with my hands.

'Hey, you okay?' asks Mike.

I twist my head to look at his black boots.

'Yeah.'

The cell door bangs after him. I walk to the table, lift the plate's lid. More fat than meat, more water than gravy. I grab the spoon and dig in. Gristle catches in the back of my throat. I cough but can't clear it. The spoon bounces off the floor. I rush towards the toilet and heave.

I take the letter from the floor, scrunch it into a jagged ball, use it to wipe my lips and drop it on my stewed bile in the toilet bowl. Then I kneel beside the toilet and rest my forehead on its cool lip.

'You thick fuck, falling for her,' says Iscariot.

He's all that's in my head now.

I hear the thud of Mike's boots approach my cell door again. I bang the toilet lid against the porcelain edge, stand up and wait.

'Time for some exercise,' says Mike.

I stare past him and walk. He closes my cell door, wheezing. The cigarettes will kill him yet. Iscariot laughs again.

'Who cares what happens to the screw? You've gone soft.'

I look at the pavement-grey sky as I step into the yard. The bloodied smell of dying cattle from the neighbouring abattoir pervades the compound air. I close my eyes and inhale. I'm a child sucking in the smell of candy floss at a circus. Hold it in my nose and taste it in my mouth. I imagine the rip of a butcher's knife as it pierces the animals' hides, their throats torn and arteries emptying warm blood onto the concrete floor of the slaughtering house. I got my taste for killing in that abattoir. Started work there when I was sixteen. But I didn't leave my work behind when I finished and it wasn't animals that Iscariot used my knife on.

'Aahh, the sweet and sour smell of death.'

Iscariot's voice electrifies my hair. I feel the roots, pulled straight from my crown all the way down the back of my skull. My eyes shoot open. I stare at Mike leaning against the wall, his jaundiced thumb and forefinger struggle with his cigarette lighter. Click, click. No flame. Click again.

I walk towards the far end of the yard, pounding the concrete.

'Christ, that screw is irritating. Can't even light a bloody cigarette,' says Iscariot.

I stick my fingers into my mouth, bear down on the flesh surrounding my nails. The smouldering fire on the floor of my stomach ignites. It spreads through every abdominal muscle then up to my chest and throat. Iscariot sledge-hammers on the inside of my skull.

The cigarette lighter clicks again. I can't bear it any longer.

My body turns, propels itself towards Mike and lunges. He falls and I'm on top of him, punching his stomach and head.

Whistles echo in the background, my fist punches harder. Footsteps close in behind me but there's no stopping Iscariot. He can't stop, he'll never stop. Not as long as there's breath in my body.

Mike's chest rattles and his dying eyes catch mine as multiple arms grab me and I'm flung on the concrete beside him. A boot lodges under my left rib. Another, under my right. Dagger pains stab my lungs. I whisper.

'Check ... mate.'

I clench my eyes shut and stop breathing. Mute velvet darkness descends.

Then I jerk, stung by Iscariot's waspy tone.

'The game's not over yet.'

SONG OF THE BIRDS — KARLA VAN VLIET

'Birds sing when they are in the sky,
they sing: "Peace, Peace, Peace".'
– Pablo Casals from his speech to the UN.

I had died the thousand small deaths
of your leaving, my heart's broken wing.

So be it. The cardinal still woke me early
with his insistent call.

And today the flocked-up blackbirds
rose, turned and opened like a fan.

What the vast blue sky requires from
me is that I leap into it.

Like the cellist said, fly, fly little ones,
sing out peace, peace, peace.

A heart can use a little peace; take it
where it comes.

I leapt.

FOR MR T
KARINA TYNAN

I will send you a Sheela-na-gig.
She will violate your stock,

Show you her immutable folds;
The fossils of your primogenitors,
Their bones.

Her gawk will speak; You have no hold
As she is young and you sir are old.

I HAVE BENT MY BODY INTO THE SHAPE OF A HARP
LIZ DOLAN

to find my way
to the love only women know

I go into the woods
to fetch water
from a well dug
into the ground

on my knees
I scoop
careful not to stir the sediment

the bucket's handle
digs ridges into my fingers

I rest

the shifting light carries me
away I return

from darkness to light
to the fullness of sun
underfoot I crush mushrooms

I worship the trees
and sing as if
they were listening.

EVERYTHING AFTER JONATHAN STARKE

A lot of people don't know this. Days after the Americans dropped the first atomic bomb, storm clouds came over the city and dropped black rain. It took hours for those clouds to swallow the sky purple, but they did. Clouds do. And we were all under them, the living with ripped cloth covering their faces to breathe, the dead in scorched cloth, unable.

I'd been sent to the well for water that morning by my father, Tojo, and heard the familiar scream of sirens as I teetered over the brick lip. I poured the water from the bucket back into the well and sat in the bucket's emptiness, afraid of the hike back to our hut. I lowered myself halfway down the well, only somewhat in darkness, and knotted the rope there where I would remain, able to see the red and orange fire bursts, the smoke float from grey to white to black. Up. Up. It went like this. Up.

And the first step I made after days in the well, after pulling myself up by that harsh-haired rope, the marks it left on me, was in ash. Slipping between my feet and the sandals, the air impossible to breathe. For a time I crawled through it against the hard earth, where man comes and goes and moves between when we are not living the breathing, aware parts of our lives. What I'm saying is, I crawled through all of this to my dead father.

Under wood timbers. Banana leaves fallen yellow between the black and the grey, fallen on Tojo's neck and hands. Facedown. Blood coming from his crooked nose. Dead. Dead eyes. The first I'd ever seen. Rolled back and yellow. This is how I found him.

When the black rain fell, I was sitting on a log far down the hill in the split-centre of the village. People were turning bodies over. They were dragging them by the hands and feet. Sometimes, body parts would snap. Come off at the joint. This stopped no one. You grab the next part. You keep pulling. The bomb taught us this.

The first black drop hit my knee. It ran down my leg like a slit of ink, dropped down from the clouds. I think I saw the dark rain first. I think I felt it first. If I hadn't, someone would have told me by now that I hadn't. *No*, they'd say. They'd say, *No*. But nobody said anything then. And nobody says anything now. But then.

Then we had nothing but fire and smoke and the billows of bodies in piles in ditches along the soft roads. And so thirsty, so hungry we all were when the first showers fell that we opened our mouths to the sky and cried against the black rain as we swallowed it down, and it filled our guts while our muscles pulled on the dead.

OLD DAY AND BIRDS — CLARE SAWTELL

Journeying in the dark
in the old day
and looking for ways to describe
blackbird's smudge at dawn,
how he moved then
took the shape of himself;
journeying with friends, some travelling,
and the lights at the sea's edge are
strung out in the wind,
– so many necklaces and hopes;
lighting candles and bits of brushwood,
turning to avoid the flashing blue lights,
taking the old road through ...

Blackbird, how you know when to sing ...
The swans are heading for the lake
beating the air resolutely
'til they get there.

ALL FOR LOVE — JOHN REINHART

I tried inverting
tried changing my skin
grew scales
grew limbs
removed the tail
tucked back tentacles
stuck my eyes to my head
opaqued my outer layer
groomed toenails
moved to a marsh nearer to her
even ate her boyfriend
wore his clothes
to no avail

| HUNGER | CHELSEA STEINAUER-SCUDDER |

Tara stares up into shifting patches of sky visible through the spires and arches of the solitary oak tree on her family's land, the only source of shade on the entire 75 acres, apart from the porch with peeling yellow paint that wraps around half the house. Today, like many August days in southwestern Oklahoma, being outside requires shade. Tara's clothes and hair are damp from the short walk across the mowed lawn, through the untended stretch of native grasses. By then, the sun has already scorched her fair skin.

The oak tree sprawls. Its roots dive in all directions into the dry soil, loyal scavengers of scarce water. Its bark is wrinkled and tough and its seams are full of stories. In it she finds the face of her grandmother. The two of them – her grandmother and this tree – bore witness to the plough coming over the last of the surrounding prairie. Saw the farm grow and then shrink, fail and then be reborn. Tara's grandfather had planted the corn, and then the cotton.

The oak's gnarled branches are raised toward the sky, praising and swaying like her mother's church friends. Some bow heavily down to the ground, resting briefly in the grass, before turning back up at the last minute to meet the scorching light.

Since she was a child, Tara has a recurring dream in which she is lying on her back under this tree and she floats and sways upwards, like a leaf falling in reverse. In the dream she weaves through the branches and around the trunk for hours. In it she is at peace.

She cranes her neck back further, directing the droplets of sweat from the nape of her neck into a small creek trickling down the centre of her back. The branches sway and turn lazily above her in the thick heat. Their leaves sag and curl at the edges like the bottoms of the dirty, worn-out curtains that still hang in her childhood bedroom across the lawn. The air shifts in waves of heat above her and she sees that small patches of mistletoe have begun to make their way from the tips of the western branches toward the trunk. Not for the first time, she's unimpressed but not surprised that Oklahoma named mistletoe, a parasitic plant, as its state flower. And now this parasite is suffocating her beloved tree. Its roots are snaking into the branches, diverting the hard-earned nutrients and precious water running up and down the tree's veins into itself instead. She despises the hunger of parasites and their relentless appetite for life.

The breeze has become heavy with humidity. Tara wonders if there will be a storm. She hears the creak of the screen door across the lawn and looks up to see her mother stepping out onto the porch.

'Tara!' she hollers in the wrong direction, toward the old horse tank along the barn. Every summer, it's filled with hose water and turned into a swimming pool. Tara waits to respond, content to watch her mother for a moment longer. She is a large and happy woman who wears loud, tacky aprons, even when she's not cooking. They cinch pleasantly around her ample waist and often match her earrings. Tara is too far away to see the current one clearly, but she knows it well. It has a red and white chequered background and features a cat drinking from a bottle of wine and the words, 'Ya'll ready fur a purrrfect evenin?'

Her mom at last looks toward the tree. 'Tara! Phone for you!'

Tara walks back to the porch where her mother hands her a glass of cold lemonade and says, eyes fixed hard on the barn, 'It's Sam.'

'OK.' Tara puts on a smile and walks across the kitchen to the phone awaiting her on top of a stack of phonebooks and old magazines. Her mother walks to the sink and stands there, still and listening, gazing out the kitchen window, pretending to watch the birds play on the rusted swing set. Tara walks around the corner and into the living room.

'Hey, Sam. Wasn't expecting to hear—'

'I'm coming to fetch you tonight.' She can hear the alcohol in his voice. Thick words that tumble through the receiver. *Hell*, she thinks, *I can practically smell your breath.*

'What? I only got here yesterday. We agreed I'd stay a week.'

'I know what we agreed. Plans change. I'm coming tonight.'

'What happ—'

'Shut up, goddammit. I'll be there around eight. Be ready.'

She walks back into the kitchen to hang up the receiver and hears a faint *Bitch* curl out from the other end. It hangs in the air between her and her mother.

'Now what was that all about?' her mother asks, not turning from the sink. Tara is glad to not have to look at her. She takes a long draw of lemonade.

'Sam's coming to pick me up tonight. I guess something's come up.'

Her mother still doesn't turn. 'You only just got here. We've hardly even seen you—'

'I know it, Mama.' Tara walks over and places her hands on her mother's shoulders. They are soft and warm and she wants to bury her face in them but she doesn't. In the reflection of the window Tara sees her mother's face. It is pained and it strikes Tara that such a lovely round face was not meant to wear such harsh expressions. She hasn't seen her look haggard since her father's cancer. Tara gives each shoulder a squeeze.

'That man, Tara … we can help. You can stay with us a spell – I know your daddy's not here, but Jim loves you like you were his own. You know he does. We'd look after you. For as long as you need.'

'I'm doing fine, Mama.'

Her mother only shakes her head and wipes a tear from her cheek. After several moments, she takes a deep breath and says, 'Well, then! What would you like for supper? I can make your favourite – got everything for it. That'll be alright, Tara, won't it?'

Tara nods. 'Yes, that'll be fine. Jim's joining, I hope?'

'Wouldn't miss it. He's out on the tractor, but he'll be in.'

Tara walks back to the tree, breathing hard. The mistletoe seems to have crawled even further in the last few minutes, but she must be imagining it. The wind is picking up and she can see a haze in the distance. 'Storm's coming,' she says.

After dinner, the clouds have turned black and the air thick. The world shifts in anticipation of the approaching storm. Tara rocks in the chair on the porch as the first fat drops of rain hit the steps. It won't be long now. Like nothing else she's encountered on this earth – not like church, not like God Himself – thunderstorms have the power to transform.

One second all is still, and the next rain plummets from the sky raging like a fire, scorching the grass, bending every blade under its torrent. Whipping and lashing everything it touches. The sky quakes and the ground holds on for dear life. All the latent smells of the earth rise. Only scent could move upwards in such weather, when everything is being flattened. Soil and leaves and grass and the flowers from her mother's garden and the hot asphalt of the sidewalk and the tar of the roof. Smells that rise up like souls. If they were colours, they'd meld into something beautiful out there, the wind driving them together and then pulling them back apart, splattering and brushing them over the yard.

Thunderstorms knock the whole world out of control, turn it into something chaotic and unrecognisable. For the duration of their brief lives, storms dwarf the chaos of Tara's own and she feels free. The rain comes in sideways now and crashes against her arms and face. She stands and walks out into the yard. She's soaked in seconds and can barely keep her eyes open for the relentless stampede of water coming down upon her.

She makes her way back to the tree that is no longer a tree but a creature now, alive and wailing. It creaks and shakes, gnashes its teeth and pummels its fists. Its violence terrifies and thrills her. Lightning flashes, searing the shadows of branches into her eyes. Then the thunder, the curtain of the temple tearing in two, the earth splitting. The Gospel writers must have spent time in the Midwest.

Another rumble in the distance, but not thunder this time. Tyres on gravel. She sees the headlights of Sam's truck, blurred through curtains of rain. He parks but does not get out. Only honks the horn. Honks it again.

She could stay with the tree. She could climb it and open her face to the sky in a silent scream, calling on the rain to drown her. Or simply lie down along a branch and allow the bark to grow around her, let the mistletoe crawl over her and feed on her blood and bones. Become unreachable.

But she knows she'll go to the truck. She'll get in and she'll be angry, or she won't want to start a fight, or she'll ask to please stay. Yes, she'll ask to stay. That'll be alright. If she asks nicely, he might say yes.

Let me stay a little longer. Let me stay just until the storm passes.

But even from this distance, he's so hungry he's eaten up all her words.

CHILD PROOF — SHANNON QUINN

Thin cloth of madness
is not tethered to our DNA
and Sunday is a lovely thing.
Blood on the plate
classical music on the radio
glass of tomato juice whether you like it or not.
Hush
not here for long
not as we know it.

Let's code our future in pictograms.
I see you huddled
with your young in first snow.
I'm a shadow puppet or something
that feeds on sunlight and grass.
Or snow
what if we were snow?
Think of how many sisters we would have
what we could borrow
what we would learn.

AT A CINEMA NEAR YOU   GARY ALLEN

It's like films with alternative endings
you feel you've been had
that the director couldn't be bothered
to see it through to the finish

like the boy who walked into The World of Ice Cream
on the Lisburn Road, waited his turn
asked for chocolate chip, then shot the part-time RUC man
four times, the bullets zigzagging
round his body looking for an exit
the Raspberry Ripple, wafers, and blood
swimming on the floor like a new ending

or the old familiar one of dirty wars
and double agents, and the high-rise hotels of Spain.

I want to believe that Roswell Man exists too
that somewhere in the universe, someone is missing him
and hopes to meet again in another dimension.

I want to be the soul of the girl in the traffic accident
caught on camera as it left her body
and confused to a shadow, moved around its lifeless self
or the girl in the open casket with a headdress of flowers
who opened her eyes wide for a moment
and terrified the mourners, before closing them for good.

THE DARK IS NEVER A MURMUR
SIMON ANTON DIEGO BAENA

whenever I finger the shrapnel
whenever the projectile digs further

I know the parable of wells,
of jars, holding the bones in the east
the crow – night itself engraved on my forehead

so tell me, how
can I reclaim the light lost in winter?

There used to be
that howling at the full moon
that stillness nerves usually cling to

I need to carry the wheat,
carefully, to their gaping beaks

I did not even offer a single candle
to the stone altar in the mud

TROUBLE CROSSING THE BRIDGE   DIANA POWELL

'Soon, I will be falling. Not the crumpled collapse of a Woolworths pocket-money toy; nor the glairy smasshh! of a nursery-rhyme egg. But the languorous, somersaulting descent of the angel-boy, who foolishly flew too close to the sun. Or just down, down, down.'

This is what she's supposed to say, what call-me-Joe wants to hear, as he sits opposite, in his granny-knit cardigan, holding her life in a brown manila folder. And then he will save her, reach out his arm and save her from the troll who hides under the bridge, waiting for her to fall.

Instead, Lena's telling him about the toy. The story slips down the synapses of her brain, trips off her tongue, as easy as *once-upon-a-time*.

'A wooden cat, found in the bottom of my Christmas stocking, along with a mouldering tangerine and a handful of nuts! A cat on a drum, hiding a button beneath. "You have to press *there*," Ella told me, snatching it away.'

And the cat, proud, poised, taut as any Egyptian god, fell helplessly down until her sister let go, springing it back up. They both laughed. 'My turn,' she, Lena, cried. Then it was up/down, up/down, until her thumb faltered, and Ella grew bored and wandered away. Later, 'I saw how fine lengths of thread passed through its hollow limbs. I snipped each one with my mother's sewing-scissors.' The cat fell apart for good.

She likes to tell about the cat; she told it to all the other kindly listeners, desperate for something to add to her file. File/Life – she likes that, too. A mistake to tell about the scissors, perhaps.

And she tells Joe about Humpty Dumpty. Why not? And all those other precarious nursery-rhyme characters. The Grand Old Duke, Jack and Jill, all climbing or tumbling, unable or unwilling to be happy on flat, solid ground. These were the ones her mother favoured – no sweet baa-lambs, or garden-girls for her. Still, it was her mother's single effort at entertaining her daughters, reciting the verses over, as if simple rhyming repetition was all she could manage. No mimicry, no performance – just a clenched grin forcing out each laboured syllable between her teeth. Had-A-Great-Fall.

It was left to her father to weave words of winding fairy-stories into her ear, binding her with their spells. To take her on his lap, and tell her enchanting tales of distant lands, where magic carpets flew through the air, along with boys with waxen wings, and white horses with golden horns – 'Whooshhh! Swisshh! Abracadabra!' There were stories from her own land, too, where genies turned into witches, Ali-babas into fairies, Argonauts into Arthur's knights. And the minotaur/giant/Cyclops became the troll, who jumped out from cupboards, curtains and doors, arms swinging, fol-di-rol-ing/I'm a troll-ing.

'In the beginning …' In the beginning, she and her sister would squeal with delight and run to their rooms. But soon the tales grew dark, so he must tuck her up in bed, then move in beside her. Succubi and incubi able to tease their way through unseen crevices in window-frames. Ghosts sidling through stone walls, two feet deep. She had thought the night-time sound scratching at her ears was no more than spiders rummaging through the plaster. But no. 'They do things to you. The monsters come into your room and do things to you.' She knew that; she had seen them. Or one at least. It had the face of the troll.

DON'T TELL. SOMETHING BAD WILL HAPPEN IF YOU TELL. BESIDES, NO-ONE WILL BELIEVE YOU. DON'T TELL, EVER.

She knows she should tell call-me-Joe about the troll, as he crinkles his face at her, makes clucking noises, and cleans his square, black spectacles, with the hem of his cardigan. 'Wool is no good for that,' she wants to tell him, just as she wants to tell him about the troll. He deserves to know. And it's what he wants to hear – not about a falling cat, or childish rhymes. And if she tells him, he may see things differently, and not speak of bridges broken inside her head.

'The problem is *there*,' he says, as he pulls books pell-mell from the shelf, spreading a ream of brains onto his desk. Spongy, corrugated grey matter magicked into rainbow-coloured daubs; a microscopic journey into a forest of trees, branches, twigs. A slice of brain transformed into stepped lines ... more ups and downs; more greens, blues, reds. And here is one like hers, opened out and pushed towards her, a hemisphere on each side. '*There*' is a filament lost between the fold of the page, between the two halves of her mind. Lost in Latin words and medical jargon. 'Bridge is easier,' he explains. 'Think of it as if something is stopping traffic crossing over a bridge.'

'That may be why you hear things, see things.'

Or maybe not.

She has to enter the white tunnel now. To lie there, unmoving, filling her mind with its sound. 'We can be sure then. The corpus callosum will show up on the image.' Amygdala/orbitofrontal/medial cerebral' – another rhyme to play through her head.

Yet of course, he was right, there *was* a bridge. It was where trolls lived, after all, when they weren't jumping from cupboards, or creeping into your room. ('Under the rickety bridge,' her father had sung. 'He'll eat you for supper!') They hid under the arches, lost in shadows, waiting for unwary travellers to pass by. Or just those they knew.

She could see this real bridge clearly, where it lay no more than a giant's spitting distance from their home. She and her sister crossed it every day to get to school. A high bridge. 'High' mattered.

'There's a place ... ' she tells Joe. Perhaps if she gives him this, he won't turn her mind into a picture, to be pored over, twisted into words and slotted into the file. '... beside the water. Trees on the bank, mountains behind. A place where ...' Say it, say it, but she can't. A slip in those synapses, a trip in her tongue? Or just YOU SEE! THAT'S WHAT HAPPENS WHEN YOU TELL! I TOLD YOU SOMETHING BAD WOULD HAPPEN. IT'S YOUR FAULT. REMEMBER! SO DON'T TELL AGAIN!

'Yes!' Joe's voice jumps in, between her thoughts and words/*his* thoughts and words, triumphant. 'There are often places where the voices are heard more distinctly, the imagined echoing the real. Sometimes it helps to revisit them, and accept them for what they are.'

Maybe. Perhaps. Or maybe not.

Still, here she is, doing what she was told, like a good girl, as she'd always been, until ... Back where she has never been 'back' before, sitting on a bench above the river, waiting for the voice to come.

She had arrived at sunrise. She wanted it to be quiet, so she could hear better.

('All the better to hear you with' – another tale he had spun. He was the wolf, of course, under the bedclothes.) Behind her are the mountains, where they had lived, along with the giants, and all the other treacherous creatures. Ahead is Life/File – one or other; or neither. All she has to do is cross the bridge to whichever it is going to be. Eeny-meeny – another game they had played. Ella/Lena, Lena/Ella, until Ella was too old for such things.

And now she hears him, singing in her handbag, demanding to speak to her in no more than a hundred and forty characters. Somewhere down below are the arches, where the voice should be coming from, the troll should be living. The children's bogey-man, long-haired, goggle-eyed and long-armed. But the shadows are empty.

Trolls are different now. You find them in different places. They follow you on the magic web, creeping unseen into your life, along endless lengths of fibres. Into your home. Into your phone. That's where he is now, chirping like a bird. That's what he's been doing, ever since he returned.

GOLDEN GATE, HUMBER, CLIFTON SUSPENSION.
SYDNEY HARBOUR, BOSPHORUS, TUIRA.
NANJING YANGTZE, SUNSHINE SKYWAY…

Sunshine Skyway – as if, going up, you could reach the brightest star, while 'down' spelled certain doom. Wasn't that the fate of the angel-boy in the tales from far-away lands? Wasn't that the fate of …

TWO HUNDRED AND FORTY-FIVE FEET ABOVE THE FLOWER CITY'S HARBOUR.
FOUR SECONDS TO HIT THE WATER, SEVENTY-FIVE MILES AN HOUR.

So the boy's descent hadn't been slow, after all! And there had been no gentle welcoming, no waves waiting to open their arms and gather him close, as she had liked to imagine.

TWELVE HUNDRED AND EIGHTEEN BEFORE THEY STOPPED COUNTING.
THE FIRST, TEN WEEKS AFTER ITS OPENING.
TEN IN A MONTH, THE HIGHEST TALLY.

All those lives lost, all those broken people ...

... BROKEN BY THE FALL, LIMBS, NECKS FRACTURED, ORGANS RUPTURED.
CRACK. SMASHHH!

And there she is, in the water beneath Lena, who stands, now, half way across the bridge. Her mother, waving to her. And there she is, disappearing beneath the surface, down/up again, like the foolish toy, or the Duke's ten thousand men. Until she doesn't come up anymore.

AND THERE SHE IS, ON THE BANK, TENDRILS OF WEEDS FOR HER HAIR, EYES EMPTY. HER NECK TWISTED ONE WAY, HER LEG STRAIGHT OUT FROM HER BODY.

No!

YES! HAD·A·GREAT·FALL!

'Shut up! Shut up!'

BLACK AND BLUE, STREAKED WITH RED, HER HEAD CRUSHED LIKE HER PATHETIC NURSERY·RHYME EGG. HER BONES AS DISLOCATED AS THAT CAT!

Shut up, shut up, shut up!

'LIKE YOU DIDN'T DO! I TOLD YOU NOT TO TELL. BUT YOU DID, DIDN'T YOU? YOU TOLD HER. AND LOOK

WHAT HAPPENED NEXT!

Lena takes a step forward towards the edge. She feels the words wind themselves around her, just as they used to do, pulling her further, out into the breeze.

COME ON, YOU CAN DO IT. ANOTHER STEP, THEN ANOTHER. AND THEN YOU'LL BE BACK WITH HER.

She takes another step. Gaping mouths sweep past her in car windows, without stopping.

BARRIERS BUILT, TO TRY AND SAVE THEM.
ONE HUNDRED AND EIGHTEEN TALKED DOWN BY DO-GOODERS.
BUT WHERE'S THE FUN IN THAT?

She is Humpty Dumpty, struggling to stay on his wall. She is Jill, poised between tumbling after Jack, or keeping to the safe, straight path. She is her mother, knowing her daughter is telling the truth, swaying back and fore, until Lena is sure she will fall to the floor. She is her mother standing where Lena is standing now, unable to stay on firm solid ground any longer.

DON'T DISOBEY, LIKE THE ANGEL-BOY! HE SHOULD HAVE LISTENED TO HIS FATHER! YOU SHOULD HAVE LISTENED TO YOUR FATHER. LISTEN NOW!

No!

YES! HURRY! THINK OF IT AS FLYING! JUMP!
FLEE! FLY! FO! FUM! REMEMBER THAT ONE?

And yes, she would like to fly, free like the birds. 'Did you know that birds are like the Woolworths cat?' she wanted to tell Joe. 'They have air cavities in their bones. Pneumatisation, it's called.' But she was afraid of another black mark in the file.

Ella had flown, too. A different kind of flight, in a big white bird to another land.

And then her father, escaping the questions that would be asked, after her mother had leapt into the sky.

Until the day her phone had rung, and the bird had sung. Tweet, tweet, tweet.

Joe doesn't know. The white tunnel doesn't show such things. Talking doesn't tell such things, if you don't say. So it's not his fault he thinks there's something wrong with her brain; that it, along with her personality, are split in two. And yet, 'You don't have to listen to the voices,' he told her, when she said she would visit the bridge. 'No matter how strong, or how insistent. You don't have to listen at all!'

Eeny, meeny, miny, mo ...

Eeeny, meeny, troll or Joe.

Lena takes the phone, throws it high into the air. Up, up towards the sun. Then down it comes, somersaulting, down, down. A languorous descent.

She walks on across the bridge.

THIS TERRAIN   CHRISTINE PACYK

Light pollution invites early spring. Above
roadway rumble, on overhead lines,
city birds gather to sing off key. The last ash sighs
ultrasonic bubbles of distress.
In fluorescent rooms, we are not speaking
again, driving the birds' throat-speak
higher. Is this the clamour
of our uncoupling? I will not yet name this
a tragedy, so I unleash wolves
that shift shorelines and summon forests.
They dart in shadows across our skin,
filling the fissures between us.
Willow and aspen sprout in their tracks
and roots meander among organs.
I carve them into wooden houses – this city
begins. The pack weaves through new landscape,
its collective howl pulsing and permanent.
A songbird lands on my sturdiest branch
and releases a note. I summon you.
I trace your body, a wild and unknown
terrain. I hold you in all my little houses.

THE CARRINGTON CHIMNEY — MARK O'FLYNN

From the radius of any vantage point
you can see it pointing out the ransacked stars
like an angry finger of our times.
From miles away it tells you where you are not
as you orbit the streets like a dancing bee.
A fringe of sticky-weed decorates the top like a Caesar
wig, or the moss around a catfish's gills,
or the hairs of a witche's wart, though
sometimes, it must be said, a chimney
is just a chimney.
   Once it fevered out power and light
fuelled by coal and historical ambition,
bringing civilisation to its knees in wonder.
Brick by brick its octagonal tower
rises to the low-flying mist, its hollow throat
empty but for the visitations of birds
with their casual plans for the future.
Inside the spire's weight tapers upward
a column of black air, echoing the ghosts of progress,
the daylight stars in the darkness of its diminishing.
That so much weight can defy the earth
making the distance and all it contains
look up.

SOUTHERN SKIES — MARK MULLEE

On your first night with the couple, they served you hot
chamomile tea with too much honey and no teaspoon.
In the silence of the radio switched off, you stripped
and slipped into bed. You woke when you heard the kettle boil
and, in morning clothes, heard them fuss over rotting chard

and rocket in that square of cigarette-deadened soil
outside the kitchen window. On your second night, the charred
cinderblock where they rubbed their cigarette butts tripped you
in the dark, stretching up at the unfamiliar moon,
and your falling body rubbed out half their plot

MOLE — ELIZABETH MORTON

It starts with a freckle.
It is in the wrong place, you see.
You'll watch commercials for Mole Maps
and make gentle notes.
Is it an irregular form,
the shape of Kazakhstan or maybe Mongolia?
Is it pedunculated? Has it an obelisk
with a copper plaque remonstrating war?
Is it globular; a series of troglodytes
with skinny dogs in the doorways?
Is it raised, like El Alto, hovering above railyards
and airfields like an hypoxic God?
Is it a black hole haloed in white?
It is in the wrong place, that's all.
You drink black tea to calm down.
You Google moles.
Your left eye is a hummingbird, quivering.
MD Online wants you to be more specific.
Is it an undulating coral coastline,
with palm trees inland?
Is it the sort of place you'd honeymoon,
with lagoons and sea mammals?
Is it a dead end? Is it brown,
at the Detention Centre, with jandals
and a mouthful of ricepuffs?
Is it irregular?
Or does it remind you of the photocopier's
grey aura? Is it Ground Zero?
Is it the sort of place they'd burn,
the sort of place they'd smoke you out?
It is in the wrong place, you see.
It starts with a freckle.

UNTIL THE CALL COMES   GERALDINE MILLS

Donal is hauling fresh glasses out of the washer. Steam rises and catches his throat as Coady hands him the phone. He clasps it between his shoulder and his ear, all the while stacking the tumblers one on top of the other. His sister, Valerie, barely able to speak.

Their mother.

Dead.

The word sounds like a fly trying to get out the window and his father begging him to come home for the funeral. He knows he should be able to give him the answer he's looking for but he cannot.

There is no 'yes'.

Coady stares at him, 'You all right, Irish?'

'Sure, just a bit of bother at home. Nothing that won't be sorted in three or four days,' and he starts pulling fresh beers, the bar wedged with bodies as if they had come from the desert, parched. They like Donal, his accent that he slathers on, butter-thick. They give him extra tips just to hear him say 'Get up the garden', or 'fillum'. As long as they keep the dollars coming he'll oblige.

He works on into the night, keeping his sister's shattered voice at arm's-length. Then falling into bed with tiredness. No registering the bridge between sleep and wake until late morning when Mrs Kurowski starts hitting her side of the wall with her walking stick and he jumps. The phone call and its import comes tumbling in on top of him and he tries to block it out by filling his mind with the rumble of the air-conditioning stuck in the window. It makes no difference to the mugginess in the room, makes him claustrophobic in his own skin. Then outside: alarms, cop cars that *nenaw-newaw* somewhere down the block in this city, this city, where lives flicker on the snag of a fingertip.

He misses Sarah more than ever now. Sarah with her need to be reminded of home. That's all he was to her, a souvenir of rain on her face and the taste of cheese and onion crisps. She cried the last time she was with him. In her little wine-coloured hat she beat her knuckles off the wall until they bled; kicked the bedclothes onto the floor and shouted she was going back. She had enough of it all. He had always promised himself if it broke up between them then he would go back, too.

But it did.

And he didn't.

He pulls on his jeans, tee-shirt – black to keep the grime hidden – then out the door with a bite from a stale bagel, chalk in his mouth.

He nearly trips on the pile of *garbage* Mrs Kurowski has left at his front door. She's playing her spiteful games again, making trouble for him with the janitor. As soon as the elevator gates scrunch open he's in like a shot; gone before she gets to scream at him, with a face on her like a party that everyone has left, shouting that she'll call the cops on him. It's the last thing he wants: cops coming around.

The day's heat is a welder's arc on the pavement as he hurries along. Cab drivers peel rubber; a plane snail-blazes up above the skyscrapers, all gleaming flash and neon.

He has a whole morning and afternoon to fill before the call comes so he plays a little game to distract himself: Spot the Illegals. The man sweeping the sidewalk looks like Tom Henry from the far side of his own village. Donal could be his son. Then the woman with raven hair, dark skin, shorts, tight-ass pink, sparkling pockets.

Mexican?

Puerto Rican?

He can't tell.

The construction workers sitting on scaffolding sucking on their beers? Sunburnt skin, freckles, do they have a visa?

The ache comes flooding up by the time he has walked the length of another *walk, don't walk* street. It's such a cliché, this iPhone-touch city. Has given itself away to Hollywood, sold itself for the big screen. He's seen it all before on *NYPD Blue, CSI:NY*. Bag ladies, pushing their homes in shopping trolleys. Gucci bags carrying excuses for dogs; cars so close together, they would never make it in a video game.

He is at a loss for the sound of the sea, the smell of oar-weed, sanderlings rumbling along the waves, their busy little black legs imprinting the shore.

He walks block after block. When he first came he named them like the fields at home. The Dark Meadow; The Speckled Field; The High Garden. Gone soft he was on the names he had known all his life, his father showing him what one day would be his, and Donal telling himself that he had greater ideas for himself than the Bog Field.

Grabbing a coffee *to go* he heads towards the *Laundromat*, a pulsing blue light searing along the street.

It's a passing-time job. He washes the smell of stale beer out of his shirts, jeans. Big, black men folding their jocks, their comforters, chat to one another as they put them in their holdalls. Donal can tell, back from deployment, the army stamped into them. He has promised himself that when he becomes the writer he wants to become he'll write all this down. He can't give up now. He was so sure he had nailed that internship. Never expected they'd let him go. But the break will come. It has to. Then he can leave the pub with its puke and its fights and stale beer.

Of course he could have gone home when the visa was up, with Sarah. While he was still legal. But right now it's the best excuse for not going back. Unless the choice is taken from him he's not going to forsake that big opportunity that's going to come along. He has sent out so many samples of his work, applied for another internship that Coady told him about. He's heard nothing yet but no news and all that.

His sister Skypes after four, his time. The kitchen is full of mourners, curtains drawn on the evening, everyone sitting around drinking enough tea to give themselves ulcers. Valerie moves his mother's laptop to the brand new sittingroom where she is laid out. His father leans into the coffin, holding on to one of the brass handles, the waxy look on his mother's face, the glasses too big on her nose.

Up to this it was his mother who Skyped him. As sacrosanct as Mass, he would hear the dingle of the computer and he still trying to get the beery sleep out of his eyes. She switched on after herself and his father had the Sunday dinner, dishes all cleared away, table wiped down. She had a habit of taking off her glasses so she'd look good for the webcam, staring sort of blindly at him. Then she walked the laptop round the room, stopping at his father who snoozed on the couch, still with his cap on. She'd wake him up and Donal would have a few words with him. Now that they didn't breathe the same air they could be civil, the separation of the screen enough to bring them together while keeping them at a distance.

His mother would have been livid with the colour and wood of the coffin, the forest that was killed for it. Too dark, too expensive. She would have wanted one of them baskety types, eco-friendly. Her husband believing, too late, that the more money he spent on her funeral the more pleased she would have been, and he the one who would have had her knitting in the dark to save electricity.

The back of someone's head fills the screen, there is the clatter of voices, a hand reaching out for more whiskey, currant cake, the dog in under the chair, its head in its paws. The voice of his sister is calling a slow steady stream of neighbours to talk to him: Minnie Keely from the Brock, with a big horse of a face looking at the screen and mouthing 'sorry for your troubles', Tim Tiny, wringing his hands and staring above the screen for fear he might have to look at him, repeating like the chorus of a song, 'that you never miss your mother till she's gone'.

Mrs Delaney asks all the questions, greedy to be the first with the news. The lies form before he says a word.

'Yea, doing real good. Newspaper very happy with me.'

She pushes into the screen and her face fills the whole space, red with anticipation. Is he not afraid what your man with the straw hair, the president-elect, with the skinny wife might do with the undocu ... illegals?

'He's all talk,' he says to her. 'He has bigger things to worry about.'

So much for his mother's prayers that the politicians would settle it. What used she say? 'Didn't the Irish build the country, the subway, doesn't our cathedral have a mosaic to the president in the wall. Isn't there Irish blood in all of them?' Now he was nervous. Anything could happen.

Someone is keening the rosary to a swarm of bee people in the room.

'Mother most amiable, mother most admirable, mother most powerful.'

Mrs Delaney moves beyond the screen, her skirt now tighter for glutting on his story as she goes to spread salad cream on the egg sandwiches, make more tea.

And his sister comes on. 'You'll have to come home, Donal, you have to,' she pleads. 'What with me so far away, Dad can't be left on his own. Would you not come even for a little while? Or with the way things are there, come altogether; you could go back to college. Do a master's. This place will always be yours. I'm sure Dad ...'

To be back at home with his father. Not happening. The two of them rattling around a house that was never big enough for them even with the new extension. He couldn't do that. Maybe if it was the other way around, maybe if his father had split his skull in the quarry or ...

But no! He couldn't go back to what he had run from. Give him a week and his father would be back with the same ding-dong. How he'd never amount to much, his mother having made him too soft, letting him scribble *ráiméis* up in the room like a pansy. Nothing that a wet summer in the quarry wouldn't have knocked out of him. What had he said to him the morning he was heading for the plane? That his son didn't have the backbone, the balls.

One of these days that bitter man would eat his words. Donal would get a job in the *New York Times* and then his father would have something to really crow about to his pals when he went into Flaherty's for a bit of Wavin piping or sheep nuts.

'The priest'll be along soon. You'll want to stay for the prayers,' his sister says. He is saved from answering because without warning her voice begins to bubble, the screen to fade, break up. The domestic scene fragments, transforms into a cubist painting all squares and rectangles, Braque or Picasso. Then it freezes, and mouths fall open as if they've had strokes, the lot of them.

The computer chings, its signal gurgling like water down a kitchen drain. The whole room collapses and all he's left with is a postage-stamp picture of his mother, in the middle of the screen, frozen.

I WANT YOU MORE THAN PEACE OR QUIET SLEEP
LISA MORRIS

I want you more than peace or quiet sleep.
I burn away, a tribute to your name;
it costs me only tears if I should weep.

I thought that once the joy of life I'd keep,
but lost it all to love's avenging flame;
I want you more than peace or quiet sleep.

The waves took all my castles in their sweep;
I said that I alone should take the blame;
it costs me only tears if I should weep.

The dreams I built lay scattered in wet heaps,
I couldn't pull to heart my body's claim;
I want you more than peace or quiet sleep.

They say what's sown at last grows up to reap.
My love was never faultless, calm, or tame;
it costs me only tears if I should weep.

Around your chest my tendernesses creep,
we love with love that hurt the place it came.
I want you more than peace or quiet sleep;
it costs me only tears if I should weep.

CORPS DE BALLET   JAMES MARTYN JOYCE

When you said that with his legs,
my grandson could be a ballet dancer,
I saw graves open on the low slope
of the New Cemetery,
ancestors grip the clay edge,
bone hands hauling them up,
heard them snap pale fingers,
rattle knuckles on bare ribs,
before skipping, childlike, downhill,
arm in bleached arm, bony knees askew,
fixed grins on their chalk faces,
their fleshless mouths struggling,
stumbling the words:
tombé, plié, pas-de-deux.

TAKING OFF THE MASK   BRENDA DONOGHUE

She wears brown lipstick. You watch mesmerised as she applies it, without any mirror, in a lecture about parasites, ticks and fleas. Everyone leaves twitching. Boys pull their collars away from their necks; girls undo their ponytails and shake their hair free. Except her, she walks from the lecture theatre ponytail intact. She swings her rucksack on to one shoulder, it is the colour of milky coffee. She picked it up on a trip to Milan, with Mummy.

Later in the Main Rest everyone is talking about the lecture and the slides and how disgusting bloodsuckers are.

'Did you see the jaws on that thing?' Danny Ryan says. 'It was the f—king spit of Conor last night, tearing the neck off Bríd.' Conor blushes and turns his face down to his screen, but you see his smile. Danny Ryan is the captain of the college rugby team. His shoulders and arms are huge, and his head reminds you of the square timber mallet your father uses to beat dents from metal. His head sits straight on to his shoulders and he has no neck. This is causing him some bother, this no-neck of his. He was twisting his head right, then left, up, then down, in the library yesterday. You could hear click, crack, crunch, click, crack, crunch. It was disgusting to listen to. He didn't care, there was no-one important there to disturb. Maybe someone tried to pull his big mallet head off his shoulders.

They pull iPhones from coats and bags, you keep your Samsung hidden in your sleeve. They check Facebook. You are friends on Facebook, you can see their Snapchat stories, comment on their Instagram posts, but you are not on any of the group chats.

'Look on the beak on that one, jeez look at those zits, nah, loser, nah.'

Danny is checking girls on Tinder, swiping left for loser. Conor grabs his phone and with a few quick flicks right tells four unfortunate girls that Danny Ryan thinks they're cool. The boys struggle and grunt, Conor's left foot shoots out of the squirming mess and sends the Milan rucksack straight on to your lap. The leather is so soft when it brushes your skin it feels like a caress.

They are city kids. They are privileged, entitled. The boys wear Superdry or Helly Hansen, whatever shows of their ski tan to best effect. You remain silent. You are waiting, watching like David Attenborough in the field, making notes deciphering actions. They don't know you have had fleas come live in your bed because you leave your window open for the cat. Better the company of a fickle feline than none at all. They don't know you have had ticks bury their jaws in your ankle for a satisfying meal of your blood simply because you walked through a meadow of warm grass on a summer evening. They have not been wrenched from the comfort of home to live in a bedsit to attend a college sixty-five miles from home.

She of the brown lipstick, Grace O'Connor, is also silent, she chooses not to get involved in the infantile insult-slinging tournament. The boys behave the same every day; the first few times you thought it funny, now it's just tiresome. You find it tiresome because she finds it tiresome. A surprisingly accurate inaccurate throw misses Danny completely and hits Grace right in the mouth; she's really annoyed and grabs her rucksack from your lap and with a tight 'I'll see you tomorrow' storms out. Conor's half-smirking, half-stammering apology floats over her unfinished coffee, her brown glittering lip print is stencilled on the cup.

Her lipstick falls on to the greasy floor; no-one notices so you drag it under your seat and slip it inside your runner. Later, you try it on, but it makes you look stupid. You wipe it off and it leaves a glittery, muddy splodge on the back of your hand. It made Grace look exotic, it made her eyes dark and her hair glow.

You have black hair, blue eyes, white skin on a round face. Your sister Fiona says you look like a child's drawing on a paper plate. She knows about colour and light. She is taking a fine arts degree by night. She resents you making it in to college. She calls you 'brainiak' and 'fatso' depending on how she wants to send the hurt home. She resents you winning a scholarship which pays your fees and a living allowance. She has to fund her studies by working as a beauty consultant (pushing expensive cosmetics on customers). She resents you sharing her space. You sleep on a camp bed designed for seven-year-old boy scouts, it sits about six inches off the floor and creaks every time you move. Your father fitted it with castors and you slide it under Fiona's bed every morning. The bedsit is for single occupancy, you are a secret. You are supposed to hide from the landlord. Your mother thinks this is a good idea.

Daddy O'Connor drives her to college every morning in his black Mercedes E class, 161 reg with tan leather interiors. The upholstery cups her blonde head as though it was a trophy. This morning she is wearing chocolate-coloured chinos slung low on her hips and a buttermilk cashmere jumper that flows over her shoulders and arms softening her slim body, creating curves. Today she is all energy and fizz because they are going to Germany for Christmas.

'Mummy booked the flights last night. It's a drag going on holidays with your parents, I mean I'm in college now for Chrissake, but it's Christmas so you kind of have to, don't you? You're so lucky. You get to live in a great apartment all by yourself. No parents, no brother, no rules only your own rules, OMG I'd love that.'

She swings her hair over her shoulder and you are blinded briefly by a blonde shower. When she strides along the pavement like this, it's hard to keep pace. You have been spending a lot of time in the Main Rest eating chips, waiting for Grace or one of the other cool city kids to sit and talk so you can listen. Sometimes you wonder if they see you at all. Like yesterday in the library, did Danny really not see you or did he choose to ignore you?

'You should come and see my apartment some time. It's really a bedsit and its cold and drab.'

'Can I really come and see it, Irene? I'd love that. How about lunchtime? I'm free until 3pm. Then the evil gaoler comes and gets me. Honestly! He's terrified I might actually have some fun while I'm in college.'

You are stunned, she used your name. You thought she had no idea who you were. You are flattered and even though you have lectures you should attend, you agree.

* * *

A fresh batch of yellow sycamore leaves have fallen on the narrow path to your apartment. They give a satisfying crunch as you walk with Grace to your front door. You reach in your pocket and realise that you've locked your front door key inside. You were running late this morning. It takes you seconds to decide you can trust her, you reach up over the front door on to the little ledge and pull out the 'for emergencies key'.

The door leads straight in to the living/sleeping/eating area. You are silently thankful for Fiona who bullies you into military-precisioned neatness. The bed is made, the breakfast nook is clear of dirty cups, the only thing not neatly stacked away is the easel. It sits inside the only window to catch the natural light.

Grace is really impressed by the paintings resting against the wall; she recognises them as studies of *Le Déjeuner sur l'erbe* by Manet, she saw the real thing in Musée d'Orsay when she went to Paris with Mummy. You don't like them because all the women are naked while all the men are fully dressed, the artist is a man. What is surprising about that?

She assumes they are your work, that you are a gifted, interesting person. You are too weak to correct her; it's a lie of omission. Grace has no idea you share this living space with Fiona. The painting on the easel is your favourite, it is a cannon shooting fireworks against a dark sky, the moon is tucked into one corner and when you look closely all the fireworks are actually tiny cannons. It's as though it's shooting different-coloured versions of itself. The work is intricate, some of the cannons are miniscule; it must have taken her hours to do. It's not finished. Fiona said it's about how we show different people different sides of ourselves or how we become different versions of ourselves each day. Think of all the energy it takes, all that acting cool, pretending to be on top of things. You know what she is talking about – you are that cannon, you live that altered state every day, you go to bed exhausted every night. Grace is not interested in the cannon.

On Monday you go to lectures exhausted. The journey home at the weekend knocked you out and you didn't sleep well when you got to the bedsit. Fiona was in a mood and nothing seemed to be in its right place or in the right order or something. It took you until one in the morning before everything was sorted and you could go to your creaky bed.

Danny Ryan shoves his mallet head towards you in the Main Rest and asks, 'Why don't you doodle on your notes? I thought people like you were always scribbling something.'

Grace says something to him about organic chemistry notes, and after some muttering back and forth he agrees and they leave for the library. She glances back at you and smiles, a reassuring smile. She is doing a pure chemistry degree and you are doing the science equivalent of hairdressing, that says on paper she is smarter than you. But you've got street smart growing up with Fiona as your older sister. You are suspicious of every smile.

It bothers you. Why did Grace want to shush him? It was a harmless comment surely? People doodle all the time, but what did he mean by people like you were always scribbling? You forget to pause at the corner and a taxi hoots and the driver shakes his fist. The air is warm for October, a soft breeze is shivering the last of the leaves from the trees, there is quite a pile gathered at your front door and it reminds you of the day you brought Grace here. You don't want to go where your thoughts have brought you. Had they been here? Drinking from your cups, looking through your things, Danny trying on your knickers over his stupid mallet head to make her laugh. You pull the brown lipstick from your pocket and fling it at the wall, it bounces off the wallpaper and lands somewhere near the window.

Friday you go home to your mother, to the sanctuary and familiarity of home. You take the 'for emergencies key' with you and you forget about Grace and Danny for a little while.

When you return on Sunday night there is a garda car, blue lights flashing on the tree trunks, outside your apartment. Fiona screams when she sees the cannon cut into tiny pieces, the masters have been slashed. You are petrified, you cannot move, you cannot think. A ban garda drapes a blanket around Fiona's shoulders. She bends as though she is going to fall but she straightens up. She has the brown lipstick in her hand.

YOUR BICYCLE   JOE CARRICK-VARTY

That morning in 1993, the lawn misting,
unkept at the wall where we'd dug the hole
for the pond that we abandoned,
your bicycle, with spokes and chain

grown through, tangled, leant by itself.
The shape it left lasted a second;
first the wheels, then the pedals
stiff and locked, rusted, stuck to the honeysuckle

curled on the frame. Might the garden be in on this?
Might you, one day, come home, step out
over the gravel, ducking the rosebush
to find nothing but the jungle I haven't weeded since?

Or might you know already
about the snail I found there, about the webs
hung between the rubber handle and the wall,
the bell full up with lichen, moss, ear-wigs,

those woodlice in the brake pedals?
The grass tugged a little, and let go with a slow rip.
Uprooted, then coiling back
into place like a fist so intent on keeping hold.

GREASE PROOFING

EMILY CULLEN

Beacons of parlour *politesse*
from days when oil slicked easily
from a man's hair to the back

and armrests of his chair; silk
purple shields of a repurposed
scarf lovingly stitched by Mam

for Dad to palm on the plush
velvet seat through the full term
of my gestation, that postpartum

time of nesting and waiting
when we upholster loose
ends as a new child arrives.

'Antimacassars were badly
needed,' he said, like one from
another era. I wondered at

the strange, syllabic word
and the meaning
I had never known before.

THREE STRONG WORDS — KATE DEMPSEY

The signal is up & down
I stalk the room, eyes on the small screen,
one bar, two bars, one bar again.
By the window, three strong.
I sit on the warm radiator & call home.

You answer, we chat
this & that
& I ask how the work is going
you say it's just the same
& go back to the problem with the TV cable.
You forget to ask about me.
You're on about the ethics of kiwi fruit
& how the gutters overflow
then say goodnight.

You still haven't asked about me.

So I don't say, I love you,
just sigh down the line & plain goodnight.
& I know you won't say you love me
because you never say you love me
unless I say it first
& that's not the same.

So I stand up from the cooling radiator
peer through the shutter at the not-yet-full moon
finger poised to disconnect
& you go & say, love you sweetie,
& everything's all right again.
That's all it takes.

IRISH MAMMIES, BEWARE

KATE ENNALS

Do you put the whiskey in before the hot water when you make Irish coffee? Siobhán couldn't remember. She decided before, mixed the instant coffee with a slug of Jameson, and peered into the glass. She remembered something about sugar. Damn! She hadn't bought sugar! Siobhán looked through the presses where sometimes a few staple goods were left behind by previous holiday makers. Yea! There was a small white packet with the recognisable GEM pink and blue script! Siobhán put in a large teaspoonful and stirred. She added hot water, squirted whipped cream on the back of a dessert spoon, and pushed it on top with her little finger. It sank into the brown watery mix, turning it into a mouldy pale brown colour. Hum, not quite what she'd hoped for.

That morning Siobhán had met her mother off the boat in Dún Laoghaire. They had driven to a cottage she had rented in Connemara to bring in the New Year. It had lashed rain all the way, accompanied by her mother's relentless grumbling. Now, installed in the kitchen, Siobhán's mother was mithering about how awful everything was. The weather was dreadful, the cottage was not what she expected, the kitchen was cold. There was nothing more her mother enjoyed than disaster. Siobhán was determined to thwart her and said she'd make her an Irish coffee. Her mother had kept saying on the journey down, how an Irish coffee would be nice, but Siobhán wouldn't break the journey. Finally her mother had insisted they buy provisions and she had bought whiskey, coffee and whipped cream. Siobhán put the coffee on the table in front of her.

'Sorry, it doesn't look great. I wasn't too sure how to make it. But I am sure it tastes okay. It's got all the right ingredients.'

Her mother peered down into the cup.

'Hum. What happened to the cream?'

'It sank. Not sure why. I'm sure it tastes grand, Mam. Try it.'

The old lady took a large greedy mouthful, swallowed and spluttered.

'Siobhán, this is not nice! What have you put in it?'

'Is it not? Let me try.'

'No, don't. It really is unpleasant. Horribly bitter. In fact, it's making me feel very sick.'

55

Her mother began to writhe in her seat. Her face turned pale. She put her wrinkled old hands to her throat and began to gasp.

'Siobhán!'

'Mam?'

Siobhán knelt down in front of her mother. She was twisting around in her chair. Her face looked horrible.

'Mam! Mam!'

Her mother stopped struggling and slumped, slipping on to Siobhán, a dead weight in her arms.

'Oh my God. Mam, mam!'

At the first bereavement session, there were six people. They sat in a circle. The facilitator asked them to introduce themselves and tell their story. Three other people were grieving for their mothers. The only man in the group was Declan. He was 32, about 5'7, had curly hair and freckles. He wore a checked shirt over a rising stomach and blue jeans. He looked nice, Siobhán thought. It would be ironic if her mother's death found her a man, finally something Siobhán could truly thank her for. Declan was the first to tell his story.

'My mother died recently. I was with her. She was suffering with Parkinson's disease and on medication. Her hands shook badly. I was making her tea. Shepherd's pie, easy for her to swallow. I put the plate in front of her. On a tray. Coronation Street was on TV. She was struggling, lifting the fork to her mouth; food was spilling everywhere. So I started to feed her. It seems I knocked the fork against her false teeth. They were pushed down into her throat. I didn't realise what had happened. I was half watching Coronation Street. She started choking. I didn't know why. The next minute she was slumped. Dead. The emergency services found her teeth halfway down her throat.

Siobhán explained that she had accidentally poisoned her mother when making her an Irish coffee on a week's holiday in Connemara and she was followed by Selina who had also lost her mother. Selina was 28. She was tiny and plump, with blonde frizzy hair. She seemed to be full of air.

'I was going back home to Wexford. Ma has a small farm there. It's where I was reared. She has just a few hens and cats now. I was back for the weekend. I was reversing in – the front yard is narrow. Leaving, it's too dangerous to reverse onto the road, so we've always reversed into the front yard from the main road. Deery, our cat, had just had her third litter. Anyway, it seems Ma saw me reversing in from the kitchen window. She saw the box of kittens on the drive. She rushed into the yard to pull the kittens out of the way. She was tiny. I didn't see her. I hit her. I didn't realise. I will never forget the feel of the bump. It was so slight, like air had gone out of a wheel, not a body. She died, in the hospital, a week later.'

'I am so sorry, Selina! This is unbelievable,' said Siobhán, with what sounded like glee. 'Three of us have killed our own mothers!'

The therapist interrupted.

'This is a bereavement counselling, not about how our loved ones died. It's about supporting each other to get through the grieving process.'

Donna, an older woman with silvery hair piled high on her head, wearing a smart trouser suit and a long silver chain, laughed nervously.

'It is strange, though. I also killed my mother.'

The people in the room turned to look at her.

'Like Siobhán, I decided to take my mother away for Christmas. We both needed a break. My father died last year and it had been tough on my mother. I was driving to Donegal. I had booked a hotel in Rathmullen. It was late. It was dark. I was tired. I was driving too fast. There was a bend in the lane. I took it too fast and lost control. Swerved across the road. The car turned. That's all I remember. We were both cut out by the emergency services. I emerged without a scratch. My mother was dead.'

The following week the therapist went through the different grieving stages: *Denial, Anger, Bargaining, Depression* and *Acceptance.* Declan, Siobhán, Selina and Donna kept quiet, leaving it to the other group members to talk of their experiences. At the close of the session, the therapist suggested that they end the group bereavement counselling.

'I don't think the group is cohesive enough. The coincidence of shared experiences between Declan, Donna, Selina and Siobhán is an issue. The four of you may find it more helpful to find a facilitator who can support your particular needs.'

The four agreed, relieved, and went to the pub to discuss exactly what they wanted from the group so that they could identify the right facilitator.

'Do we want to try to deal with our guilt?' asked Declan. 'I feel guilty, no doubt about that.'

'Yes, the guilt is terrible, particularly because I didn't like mum much,' said Siobhán. 'I worry that my subconscious made me do it.'

She saw the look of horror on Selina's face.

'But I don't really think so,' she added hurriedly.

'My mother was a Fascist,' said Donna. 'But I'm not sure I feel guilty, exactly. I do feel it was an accident.'

'I feel very guilty. My mum was lovely,' moaned Selina. 'A real sweetheart. She was just a bit soft in the head.'

'It is strange, though, isn't it?' asked Declan. 'How there were four of us in a group of seven? Do you think there are more out there?'

'What, mother killers?' said Siobhán, laughing.

They looked at each other.

'We're not mother killers,' protested Selina.

'Maybe there are more people that this has happened to than we imagine,' said Donna.

'Yeah! We should set up a network. The Dead Mothers Society!' said Siobhán, dryly.

'That's not a bad idea, Siobhán,' said Declan.

'I was joking!'

'A network might provide support, talk, whatever it is that networks do?'

'Support? How? Look at the best ways to kill disliked mothers?' Siobhán asked.

'I loved my mother!' protested Selina.

'There may be many people out there who have similar experiences,' said Donna.

'But do we want to extend our group?' asked Selina. 'I'm not sure I want to meet any more people like us.'

'I wouldn't mind meeting a man with the same experience, no offence meant or anything,' said Declan.

Nor would I, thought Siobhán.

'How do we advertise? Looking for Mother Killers? Apply within. Don't expect we'll get a huge response, except from the gardaí,' she said.

'We could invite people to an event on our Facebook pages and see what response we get.'

They agreed. Declan put up the event on Facebook. It received over 200 responses within four days. Over 100 people registered. The press got hold of the story. Declan was interviewed on RTÉ and NEAR FM. Siobhán was interviewed by the Sunday Indo. When it was published, Donna rang her.

'Siobhán, have you read this article?'

'Not yet, read it out. How do I sound?'

'*Dead Mothers Society Set Up by Child Killers*'

Irish mammies, beware! A Dead Mothers Society has been set up by four people whose mothers recently died. Each of these apparently grieving sons and daughters were involved accidentally in their mothers' deaths. They met at a bereavement counselling session and found the support and shared experience helped them overcome their loss. They have established The Dead Mothers Society after setting up a Facebook event which attracted over 500 likes. Over 200 people plan to attend the event next Saturday, 29 April.

'I don't like being labelled "child killer".'

'God knows what we've begun, Donna. Maybe the Indo is right. Irish mothers, beware!'

THE BALLAD OF CROSS-EYED KATE   JARLATH FAHY

(To the air of *Di Provenza il mar* from Verdi's *La Traviata*)

How long have I loved thee cross-eyed kate
As long as your prosthetic leg is put on straight
And your washed-out wig is at its proper angle
That arm you lost in last year's mangle
Down all the years dilapidations
Through arthritis haemorrhoids and ulcerations
After all the pain of reconstruction
I love your botox and liposuctions
I don't mind that your breath is laboured
If it wasn't cheese and onion flavoured

It's true you never stayed at home
You were always inclined to roam
Paragliding was your obsession
Between the elations and depressions
Until like Icarus you crashed into a tree
Losing your leg up to the knee
Things were never the same as they were before
As you crawled along the floor

Now every morning after eight
I set you upright on your skates
And I push with all my might
As you skate off into the light
Twenty years went by so sweet
Then you lost your buckteeth
Swinging from a trapeze
They replaced both your knees
when your hair went on fire
you got enmeshed in wire
after the oil tank exploded
driving round a bend blindfolded

THERE ARE ONLY A FEW THINGS
MARY MELVIN GEOGHEGAN

a dew drop on a leaf
the meniscus on a glass of water
the suggestion of a parabola.
Caught in a moment
with Alice Through the Looking-Glass
pretending to run
waking up the underworld.

I IMAGINE YOU AT YOUR SECRÉTAIRE — ANTON FLOYD

I imagine you at your secrétaire
all other tasks complete
as you compose this letter
words glisten on the sheet
of pale blue airmail paper
the perfect foil for navy ink
a writer and a reader's pleasure
to have a missive so distinct

your handwriting is garland style
so singularly you the finish
a paraph to grace each capital
a made-to-measure flourish

now in every cursive line you traced
I find the echo of your long-lost voice

PLUM MARKER — SHAUNA GILLIGAN

The curve of the cake almost overtakes the round of shoulder it is so sensuous.

In the kitchen, Tim watches his wife Rebecca. He listens to the scrape of the wooden spoon against the plastic of the bowl as she mixes. Round. Around. And round. A slight pause between the rounds as she gathers more ingredients: pushing the sugar into the soft mound of butter, then the fine flour slipping between the spoon and the lip of the bowl which she holds tightly.

He sits in the corner on a worn beige armchair, *The Irish Times* open on his lap, half-read, and his glasses pushed down his nose.

Tim watches Rebecca, now rinsing the plums, their oblongs shiny with water. He finds himself grimacing as she slices the centre, picks out the stone with the point of the knife.

There's a pile of stones to her right, like one of those mounds people leave in the mountains, a marker to show they were once there. Tim considers keeping the pile of plum stones before dismissing the idea; the tree is their marker. They planted that plum tree when they'd first married. And every year since, Rebecca has made their favourite plum cake, known as *Zwetschgendatschi* in Bavaria, where they'd honeymooned. Tim had written the long word into Rebecca's recipe book, opposite the instructions for plum jam.

She uses her grandmother's recipes, ones in which quantities of flour and butter are not quite right. It's to do with balance, she said the other day to Orla, their daughter. The quantities don't matter. It's the balance between dry and wet ingredients. Tim watched Orla's face as Rebecca tried to explain. Orla stormed out saying *but mum I just wanted the recipe, not a lecture.*

'All I want for that girl is happiness. Is that so difficult for her?' She'd turned to Tim, and he'd nodded at nothing, for he thought Orla happy in herself. It was Rebecca's insistence on contributing to this state of happiness that seemed to tip it over the edge or vanish it altogether, like a magic trick.

Later at the airport Orla had attempted an apology by saying she'd remember how the cake was made and that she'd look up the recipe on the internet for the finer details. It didn't matter, Rebecca said, you could use any fruit once it had the texture of plums. It would be fun to experiment with tropical fruit. Orla had smiled, saying she wasn't sure if the fruit in India could be classed as tropical, but still, she'd give it a go. That night Tim kept his fists clenched tightly by his side as he listened to Rebecca cry herself to sleep. He could never talk to her when they'd fought; she'd only accuse him of taking Orla's side and so he'd pushed himself into this neutral silence.

Tim shakes his head and returns his focus to Rebecca. Now she places the halved plums into the mixture, the colour of buttermilk. Her forefinger fits into the groove of the flesh where the stone once was. He listens to her absentminded humming, and hears the slight give of the mixture as she pushes each plum half down. She does the same with the second mixture. She always makes two cakes. He clears his throat, pushes his glasses back up on his nose, and rustles the newspaper before re-reading the main story.

There's a photograph – a still from a video of a beheading – of a man in orange, and a hooded man in black, like a shadow beside him, holding a knife to his throat. This is what marks this man's life, Tim thinks, chewing his lip. The life of a man of words remembered as pictures, on worldwide replay. He thinks of Orla, and her work with the street children in Hyderabad. Maybe she isn't so safe, after all.

'Another forty minutes or so and we can have tea and cake,' Rebecca says, her voice cheery, and forced.

'Hmm.'

Tim is aware that his response is automatic, that he has heard, but not heard, his wife. That she is not merely telling him that they can have tea and cake soon. No. She is waiting for him to thank her for preparing and mixing, washing and dissecting. But Tim knows he is not a grateful man. He wants to ask her if she thinks Orla should come home even though she's just gone back, but as he opens his mouth to speak, Rebecca shouts.

'Is this it? Is this how it's going to be? You retire and sit around, watching me, as if I'm some sort of *exhibit*. Well it's not, it's not going to be like this.'

He looks at her and sighs.

'Oh well you might sigh,' she shrieks. 'Well you might sigh while I still do all the work. The cooking, the cleaning, the baking, the laundry, the house itself. Alice's husband retired and you know what he did? Do you?'

Tim cannot bring himself to say more than '*what?*'

'I'll tell you what.'

Rebecca takes a deep breath. Tim watches how the thin lines of her ribs move beneath her light salmon-coloured top as she gets ready for the next onslaught. She has been having this conversation with him in her head, he knows. Her mouth moves just before she speaks; she has wound herself up to this point.

'Alice's husband built an extension.'

Tim glances up at the wash of bird droppings on the glass ceiling of the conservatory, wondering if it couldn't be classed as an extension. He folds the newspaper noisily. Though he doesn't want to think about the murmurs of his heart or his breathlessness, let alone talk to Rebecca about his worries, he finds himself speaking. His voice is louder than he intends.

'I think I need to buy some new clothes.' He stands and fingers his rugby shirt. Tim has had to shed almost a quarter of his body weight. His clothes hang on him, as if drying on a line. Rebecca's current silence has been her only comment. She likes neither challenges nor change.

'Do you think,' he hesitates as she stands right before him, 'do you think, Rebecca,' he tries again, 'that you might help me?'

Rebecca nods, and then covers her face with her hands. Her shoulders shudder through her sudden tears. The sky has darkened and Tim looks out, surprised at the cries of seagulls this far inland.

He turns and walks through the conservatory with its two floral sofas, the shining wooden floor, and the sound of his leather-soled tan shoes marking his steady beat. Rebecca follows him. He can feel her anger, and her sadness, mixed together, each fighting for prominence. He asks himself what his intention is. He takes a breath, and opens the back door.

Rebecca steps out into the garden with him. She's wiping her face with a tea cloth. They stand, side by side, and watch the seagulls circle over their house and back down to the plum tree, their marker. He looks at her, the silver sheen of her hair, and the dull blonde that the hairdresser has put in it. He feels that in trying to fix himself, he has somehow broken her.

'Our marker,' he says.

Rebecca's gaze moves to the remaining plums hanging between the thin green leaves, waiting to be plucked. He reaches out to take her hand. But she shakes her head, and goes back into the house.

Tim now stands at the kitchen window where he can get a good view of Rebecca. He watches her fiddle with the tea cloth, pull the cakes out of the oven and push them back in. She looks up, catches his eye, and turns away. Tim decides that, magically, the baking has brought the gulls. And he smiles, content and relieved at the slow shift in weight, and how, since his retirement his heart, though it murmurs, will become the heart he wants: a healthy one, a happy one. Intention, he asks himself again, what is my intention?

The sky brightens once more as the clouds move away without rain. Leaving the door open, he walks back inside. Rebecca, paused in motion, one foot in the kitchen, the other in the conservatory, has her hands on her hips. Her tears have dried. Tim knows that she will eat just a mouthful of cake, to taste, and the rest will go onto the patio in lumps and crumbs. She runs her hand through her hair before retreating to the safety of the kitchen. Tim stares after her, thinks of the curve of her arm, the round of her shoulder. He will kiss her cheek, he thinks. Before she takes the cakes from the oven, he will steal a kiss. And they will laugh together.

He returns to his chair and finally finishes the newspaper, his throat dry, and when he next looks up, he finds Rebecca has set the plates on the table. The primrose teapot is steaming and the cake – of course, the cake! – is already out of the oven on the wire rack. There will be no kiss, he thinks, as he watches her pour the milk from a creamer that matches both teapot and cups. He stands, and in silence pours the tea. She dishes out the cake. A large slice for her; a sliver for him.

'This time,' she says, 'you have the taster slice.'

Tim watches how her face has reddened. She knows he shouldn't eat cake. He nods, and takes a forkful. He closes his eyes, and tastes.

'Well?'

'Hmm.'

Rebecca claps her hands.

'The light sponge and the juicy plums,' he continues. 'Yes.'

'It's not as if we need an extension,' she says, standing and staring into the conservatory. 'And I believe Alice's extension wasn't as good as she had expected. He's always letting her down, that husband of hers.'

Tim does not reply. He takes another forkful of the cake and a sup of tea. Rebecca sits at the table and eats her cake, leaving not a crumb on the plate. The sky darkens. They both look towards the garden as the rain finally comes down. Sheets of perfection, Tim thinks, as he sinks back into silence.

Tonight they will Skype Orla. Rebecca will show off the remaining plum cake, untouched, and Tim will remind Orla she doesn't know what she's missing; she will say *oh but I do! Rebecca's cake!* And they will all laugh because modern technology can never take the place of taste and touch. The sun will be bright and low in the early autumn evening so they will have to move the computer from the conservatory to the front room where they can see Orla's flickering image a little more clearly. Tim will tell her how she's more and more like her mother; Rebecca will tut-tut at him. And Orla will tell them – as she always does – about the *good* work she's doing with the children. They will blow kisses into the air, the sound of wet lips travelling across continents, the steadiness of familial love.

And that night, finally knowing his intention, Tim will turn to face Rebecca in their bed that is as old as their marriage and he will tell her he loves her. He will say he is grateful. Yes. His hands will rest on the smooth round of her bare shoulders and he will tell her he is grateful that she is his wife.

PROSTITUTE — AGNIESZKA FILIPEK

on a bed made out of roses
I'll arrange my head
and tell a dream about suffering
thorns will pierce my heart
love will pour from me like blood
red petals will anoint my lips
so bitter from all your kisses
small leaves will envelop my breasts
never loved by anyone
and the memories of you will die inside me
I'll toss away withered blossoms
in the morning I'll wake up fresh again
for someone completely new

LIFE IS NOT A DANCER BARBARA DE FRANCESCHI

No Zumba rhythm keeps it fit.
Yes there are twirls and pirouettes,
pianos tinkling in the rain,
a quickstep braided into giddy spins
to avoid the one/two/threes
of a steady waltz.
We have no compass
in the depths of time,
we gasp for air,
fling our limbs into energy cycles,
try to teach intelligent thoughts to flap
like silver fins
without drowning in the mud.
Gold surges on hassled waves –
free trade and alliances.
We get hooked on the glitter.

Maybe life is a fish.

THIEF HONOR DUFF

Maytime I stole Lilac
from a wayside tree, heavy with rain,
snapped off six stems with purple flowering heads
and breathed again that special scent which brought me
down the years to youth and joy, under a perfumed tree
on Mobhi Road, kissing a boy.

After I broke its limbs,
fretted I'd left the tree in pain,
bleeding green sap, trying to heal its injuries in vain,
torn rudely from its hedgerow haven
at the whim of a thief.
Yet, I had captured beauty
and the Lilac's time is brief.

NIGHT VIGIL ON THE N7   RÍONA JUDGE MCCORMACK

On the other side of the glass, under the ticking striplights, her reflection is bloodless, papery. There are blue lines beneath the skin. She leans forward and presses one finger against her eyelid, where the vein runs like an old scar. The pulse there is skittish, flick-flicking in fluttered code. But still going.

The bathroom door swings inwards with a clatter of suitcase wheels and voices. She straightens in front of the mirror. From her bag she takes a comb, powder, a compact of rouge. Her repair work is efficient, a routine long-practised. The woman in the mirror no longer looks close to death.

'There,' she tells herself.

A sunburnt woman at the next sink turns. 'Sorry, love?'

Outside, she finds herself standing for a long, embarrassing moment before the customs signs. A foolish old woman, dithering.

Nothing to declare, reads the green channel. It seems that cannot be true.

In the concourse beyond, Johnny is waiting by the shuttered newsagent's, keys turning in his hands. He smiles when he sees her, then remembers himself.

'Missus Rourke.'

'Johnny.'

He doesn't ask about her flight. She takes her hand from the suitcase handle and he is already there, guiding it away like a small dog at his heels. They walk in silence to the parking block, the suitcase making small talk along the tiles: *snick-snick-snick-snick*.

At the car, he opens the door for her with a self-conscious flourish.

'There you go.'

'Thank you, Johnny.'

She seats herself stiffly in the passenger seat and composes her face. It is easier here, around him, to behave as is expected of her.

On the dual carriageway, already filling with early commuter traffic, the lamps on their poles cast regular pools of sickly light along the hard shoulder. In the wing mirror her reflection is lit yellow, then fades, then is lit again.

All the long way over darkened Europe she had sat with her forehead against the window, looking down. After the red-dirt heat of Adelaide it had seemed like an alien land, a place she might never have known.

Somewhere over northern France the moon had risen, blue and remote, and washed the clouds in its thin, cold light. She had wanted to cry – it had felt like the moment to do so – but she had only watched, dry-eyed, as the moon rose higher and Ireland had approached.

Out of the city, the traffic eases. The N7 unrolls out before them, smooth and black, the streetpoles thinning and then petering out into darkness.

On the dead stretch out along the golf courses, Johnny clears his throat. *Don't*, she thinks. She hears katydids singing over a yawning hole.

'Missus Rourke ...'

She turns in her seat. 'But I haven't asked yet, how is your Darragh?'

'He's grand.' Johnny brightens, takes one hand off the wheel to scratch happily at his chest. 'Grand altogether. Great little fella he is, he's started walking just this week.'

'Must be getting big now.'

'Huge. Huge legs on him, footballer legs. And he eats! Maureen says he'll have us eaten out of the house before he's grown. It's like every time I come home there's something new he's doing. I don't want to be away, now, in case I miss anything.'

She nods in the right places, encouraging. But Johnny stops, hesitating, and she closes her eyes against what is coming.

'Listen, Missus Rourke ...'

'Kathy.'

'Missus Rourke –'

'You must call me Kathy, now, Johnny. You're not in my class anymore.' She allows a certain tiredness into her voice. 'It's been a long time since any of you were.'

A car overtakes them, full beams flicking on and throwing the tangled mass of winter hedging all along the verge into high relief. Johnny clears his throat again, determined to say his piece.

'All the same, look. I just wanted to say, it's a terrible thing about Michael.'

She finds she cannot speak. There are words, but they will not come.

She wants to say: Yes, yes it is. Terrible – so full of terrors. May you never know. Instead, she says, 'These things happen. We carry on.'

In the silence, they both look back at the road, and it is then that they see the car ahead swerve and the low thunk of something being hit at speed. It happens so quickly she is not sure which comes first. Then Johnny is pumping on the brake pedal and they are almost upon it themselves, a huddled shape on the road – large, larger than a cat, or even a fox – skidding past it and towards the hedging in a long, slewing stop, in a shriek of rubber and air throbbing in her ears.

The engine cuts out and there is a sudden stillness. She can hear her own breathing, Johnny's too.

Somewhere up ahead a car door opens. Voices. Footsteps, running.

A dog? she thinks. A deer?

Johnny unclips his belt and coughs, an oddly wet sound. 'Are you alright?'

She nods, but he cannot see her. He is rolling down his window, looking back down the carriageway. 'Yes,' she says. Her voice sounds faint and uncertain.

'Wait here.'

And he is out, gone. The headlights are turned upon branches and long grasses, grey and solid. She listens to the pinging of the open driver's door.

Jesus, Jesus, Jesus, a woman's voice is saying, out there in the dark.

Johnny is back, his breathing ragged. 'I think – fuck – I think we'd better move the car back. In case anyone else comes, so they'll see.' He restarts the car and the headlights flicker, the bare branches move weirdly, shutter-stuck. Then he throws an arm around the back of her headrest and turns in his seat, reversing them back out onto the tarmac, back towards the creature and the other people standing in the road. In a single fluid motion the car swings out wide and then back into the lane, lining them up neatly so that they are pointing forward towards the people and the shape in the road.

There is a man in the headlights, lying on his side. She knows with a strange certainty that he is dead.

'Fucking Christ,' Johnny says, and then, out of some schoolroom reflex: 'Sorry, Missus Rourke.'

'You're fine,' she says. 'You're fine, Johnny.'

She will not teach again, she realises, once the term is over. She must have come to a decision on the flight back. No more minding the children of other people, correcting their faults. She will sit for a while, in the front room, and watch as the boundary hazels flower in long beards of white. She would like to leave the village, move away from everyone who knows her as Missus Rourke. But the prospect of uprooting and beginning over tires her.

He just walked into the road, the same woman's voice is saying, angry, rising into hysteria. *What was he thinking just walking into the road?*

Drunk as fuck, a male voice says, more quietly.

She closes her eyes and sees again the burial, out there in the white glare of the Australian sun. Michael's daughters, and his wife, Annie, in black sunwear; the high buzz of cicadas rising. The sunken maw of earth calling to her.

She is conscious now of a pain across her chest, where the seatbelt has cut into her. She can see them in the headlights, three of them standing above the dead man. Then Johnny steps away from the other couple and walks back towards her, hands in his coat pockets, head down against the glare of the lights.

He taps at the window and she realises that the doors have locked automatically. Through the glass his voice is strangely warped.

'It's there in the middle, the button there.'

She presses it and all four doors snick open. Johnny falls into the driver's seat, tired and sighing.

'Some old beggar, it looks like. Poor sod.' He scratches again at his chest, a habit she seems to recall from his childhood. So many children, all grown now. 'We'll have to wait. Make a statement.'

He flicks on the heating dial against the pre-dawn chill. They sit and watch over the dead man lying still in the headlights.

After a minute she unclips her own belt and opens the door. The cold is worse outside, sharpened with coming frost. Johnny is scrabbling with his own door, stumbling after her.

'Missus Rourke, come back in now, you'll freeze –'

She doesn't turn. 'Johnny, go sit in the car.' She uses the Voice, the one that can silence an uproarious classroom upon entry, and he backs away even before he understands he is doing so.

The dead man is lit by their own headlights, and the lurid red of the other car's brake lights. Blood? she thinks as she approaches. But there seems to be none – a trick of the light only.

As she reaches the body a sudden slam of air and noise and lights hits her, pushing her with a gasp to her knees. A car passing without slowing. Behind her,

Johnny's face shows pale and worried through the windscreen, so she takes long and steady breaths and rearranges her features carefully.

The pulse in her eyelid beats on: don't let them see. Not when her husband had left her all those years before, not when her only son followed. Never let them see. The faces at the windows, the parents waiting at the gate.

'You'll come visit, of course?' Annie had asked, her Adelaide inflection lifting the statement into a question.

'Of course,' she had said. And she will, though not for some years, and in the spaces between her grand-daughters will grow into people she does not know. They will never come to live with her. This had been decided without her, she had realised soon after the service, and the knowledge had struck her harder than even the news of her son's death had. She had almost asked, *what would Michael have wanted?* But there was little dignity in that.

The dead man is wearing an old, discoloured army greatcoat, wide pockets gaping like mouths. His boots are worn through at the soles. She can see socks, or dirty skin, through the holes.

There is the smell of old drink, old sweat. One arm is flung out, as if the man is warding off bad dreams, and he is sleeping, only, here on the N7 in the darkest hours before dawn.

She touches her hand to the scarf at her neck and begins to unwrap it. Kneeling in the cold, she lays it across the man's face, brushing the cashmere into place around his neck. Then she lays down beside him on the damp tarmac. Ignoring the voices, the car doors opening, she curls herself around his prone form, his greatcoat musty against her face. She wonders how it might feel in the moment before being struck.

Moon-faces stare down at her, their mouths dark holes.

The sky above is bluing into faint light. Sunrise will be coming soon, over the Curragh. She closes her eyes and once again the gaping maw of earth swims up towards her. It is a relief, this once, to let it happen.

OFF THE RECORD   MAURICE DEVITT

How I looked in tie-dye, kaftan
and desert boots, trademark vinyl
tucked under my arm. Enlivened
by nutmeg and banana skin
I dreamt of you, the seamless
stitching on your new red coat,
amoeba-patterned dress
and those thigh-high boots,
straight from *Top of the Pops*.

I waited for the slow-set,
missed a beat and found myself
changing records while you,
with sleight of hand, changed
partners so fast, I recognised
neither them nor you. I left
the party without saying goodbye,
walked home alone, dawdled
at the end of your road,
as though waiting for you to catch up.

MORNING MASS IN GALWAY   MICHAEL FARRY

I strolled the streets attempting indifference,
then slunk into the staid building between
the second-hand bookshop and city hall,
joining the lukewarm remnant of uncertain
loyalists, on edge, twitching nervously
at every squeak of leather on worn tile.

We were relieved when it started and we
could join in the familiar drill, sit, stand,
assent at the proper times. Our voices
lost in the vault mocked us, like litanies
of vain service, but street noises cheered us,
indicated we were being ignored, harmless,

our day spent, tempting us to raise voices.
After the propitious meal, assignments
and goodbyes, most lingered, slow to forsake
old comrades, shade and the sanctuary.
It could not last so one by one we left,
to flounder through exuberant streets.

SOMEWHERE NORTH OF THE PLAZA HOTEL
PADDY KEHOE

He cannot find the street again,
But it is enough to recall
The few days of solo harvest,
The pearl-grey evening,
The canticle of the returning sun
Over the wheel of the world,
Somewhere in the humid thoroughfares.

BOG

ROZZ LEWIS

Caitríona Barrett gave birth to a baby girl alone in her bedroom. When the baby died shortly after, she buried her in the bog that Jim, her father, cut turf on. The rushes shimmer here on the bogs. The strand is at the end, its greyness and dankness give nothing away. The people are content with the silence, they've always had this and they live by it. She made a grave for her baby by digging into the squelch of the bog with her hands clawed out wide. She did not dig long enough as she couldn't cope with the sounds her hands made against the warmth of the bog's insides.

I wasn't there when she did this. It's as if this is the way it happened though. I was the one who found the baby in a fluorescent pink sports bag, half buried and left, given over.

It's late morning, and the sun is up on a fine day. The road to the strand and Jim's bog is jutty and sharp. Greys and silvers of the stones cut through the bogland. The sky is an awful baby blue with candyfloss clouds.

After I made the call that evening, the gardaí questioned every young girl around here. I felt relieved having reported it when I heard on the radio that a local girl was receiving medical attention and hoped the baby would be buried properly in a graveyard. Not left out alone at the top of the strand.

I can see the bog from my house and it's summer, teacher holidays so I've no school to go to. I pull on my tracksuit and drive to the top of the strand road. The windows rolled down, the morning is heating up. The tide is out with pockets of water abandoned and stagnating on its surface. The tide forgets those always. Jim cuts one of his bogs by hand, the rest he leaves to the machines. He said it kept him fit. The area where the baby was found is taped off, the yellow Garda tape marks out a rectangle. It's one of Jim's hand-cut ones. She meant for the baby to be found. I was destined to find it and I had to complete the circle, get a thanks and be finished with it, put that baby out of my mind.

I get back into my car and drive home. I find my best suit, the one I wear to interviews, and find my shirt is unironed. I steam it and pick a dark green tie to go with it. I polish my shoes for the first time ever since I bought them. I shower and get dressed. I'll walk up to their house, the whole village will be parked up. Jim is a popular man around here. I set off on the walk up through the village to the Barrett house.

There are cars everywhere, blocking the road and the driveway. I nod to the priest on his way out. He's rushing off to ready the church.

It's terribly sad, I say.

Shocking for the village and Jim and the girl. Would have been better if —

He stops, places his hand on my shoulder.

Heading in?

I nod and he doesn't reply, gets into his car, fastens his seatbelt and reverses out.

People are odd around here. I've lived here for nine years and will never call myself a local. I was told that by one of the teachers on a night out.

You'll never be one of us, she had said. Your great grandchildren might be called locals, and we had laughed together but now it seemed like it had been a warning to me that I hadn't had the wisdom to receive. I stand at the front door, looking down at my polished shoes with the laces tied nice and tight. I smooth my shirt out before I ring the doorbell and it seems like a year before a face appears at the side window.

Go around the back, she signals, and disappears.

I walk around the back where the door is open. A few young men stand outside with a girl. The men are dressed in checked shirts and white trainers. The girl is in a black skirt and white shirt and she pulls on a cigarette while the men swig from a bottle of Budweiser. I know them.

Sir, they say and all swig their bottles. The girl does not look at me, pulls heavier on her cigarette. I step into the kitchen into a cloud of smoke. The old people are here. Plates of sandwiches and Mikado and Kimberley biscuits with bottles of whiskey and brandy cover the centre of the table. I don't know anyone, I don't go to mass and stopped going to the pub but they know me and what I found on Jim's bog.

I go through to the sitting room and where the coffin and the mourners for the baby will be. I wonder if the coffin will be closed. All I remember right now is the baby's hands. Can't remember any nails, just skin. I don't think I saw its face. I stop at the door when I see a woman I know from the shop.

How's Caitríona? And Jim?

Not good. Sure, how would you be at all? Jim saying nothing, no change there, and she's taken to the bed. Doctor Sullivan is lodged up here day and night.

What does he say?

Caitríona's body is sound but no one knows about the head. That's a hard one for the doctors even. I heard her raving about you today. Some of us are not grateful, you know, to you. It's shocking, the whole thing. You'd wonder should you be here at all.

With this, I had to get to see her or Jim. She might be able to reach out to the man who had helped her, the one who had last seen her baby. She might not speak today but at least she'd know I was there. Though I knew this wasn't about her confessing to me or relying on me. I needed to let it out, to share what I had found, why I had done what I did. We needed each other, in a way.

A fire is down in the sitting room, though it's not needed for the summer months and a strong smell of turf and smoke is making things uncomfortable. A shiny white coffin, 3 or 4 foot long. I try not to look but can see it's closed over. I wonder is the baby in there or is it to help Caitríona come to terms with it?

Some people mutter when they see me and others shuffle by the fire, sipping at their tumblers of drink. A man I don't know gets up and steers me out of the room, his fingers grip into my arm like a claw.

Leave the lot of us now, you've done your bit, he says. You came and saw and now it's good luck, Sir, and he unlocks the front door.

I scramble out. People are coming in. They look at me and I see they know me and they think the same as that man does. As if I wanted to find that bag. I did the right thing. The mother of that baby needed help but I need it too.

I take to the road with a brisk walk then a run. I need to find Jim, I know where he is, the only place he'd be. I see his car, it's parked up at the top of the strand. I take my jacket off and tie it around my waist and when I get closer he winds his window down.

Well, he says, getting out. We stand side by side, looking at the yellow taped area.

They took the bag, the lot. Have you ventured back down there since? he says to me.

I shake my head, afraid to speak. Silence is best now. Say nothing.

He looks at me for a moment then asks me if it had occurred to me to cover the blessed baby over, to leave her where she had been put. Now she'll have to go

81

into the graveyard beside my wife and her own mam, he continues. It's not right that the baby who never met my wife will take my place now. Caitríona picked this place for the baby, and he points to the yellow tape. Some things are better left unsaid.

Jim, you're not speaking sense. This is a dead baby and your daughter is unwell. It's more than just some gossip that can be brushed aside. You've to understand why I wanted to help her.

We can't and you should know that, you have been here long enough.

He looks at me, perplexed with no anger in him. He looks shrivelled as if he hasn't ever slept.

He carries on. Now, I'm just a bad father with a bad daughter who buried her baby in the bog. You know rightly how things work around here. I'll just be a two-sentence father now. And you will be the worst, I guess that's something at least. I cannot be as bad as you and neither can Caitríona. It is you that will fare the worst in these parts. What kind of man fiddles with things like this?

I breathe out deeply. The yellow tape has came loose and is flapping back, looking to escape.

I deserve thanks, I say to him. This is a messed up place but I'll stick it out. I'm not going anywhere, Jim. I can forget as well as all of you.

I break away and leave him looking at me and I go down the strand road. The tide is on the way back in, the weather is taking a turn, the rain will come soon and it will wash the bog down again. It will drip into the water and tomorrow will be dark and dank and awful. I reach the yellow tape and pull at it. It flies across the bog, hopping and bouncing its way onto the strand where the tide can claim it, hopefully send it out to the Atlantic and away from here.

Jim's car is reversing away up the road and I am alone so I kneel down on the side of the bog opening and look right into it. The gardaí have taken everything, there is not a bone or nail or hand. I dig into the bog, get my hands rightly dirty and wet and it makes a squelching noise. I take a fistful of the wet bog and squeeze it tight and release it. It falls in a hump in the middle of the bog. I go right into the middle of it and pull more and more bog out, my white cuffs filthy, and I feel the heat of it on my hands. I want to stuff it right into my eyeballs but my eyes are crying and I can't close them forever.

I still can't remember much of that day or if I even saw the baby's face or even a hand. I decide the baby was compressed with love into the bag, the zip pulled up and I decide that I will remember her one way only. I smooth the bog over afterwards, like there is nothing there but bog and like there was never anything there before. Sometimes, things are better left sitting like those tidepools and when the tide has gone out, the water in the pools is cool and dark green and you can't dream of putting your foot into it as there'd be no bottom.

SUMMER IS COLT FAST   GERRY STEWART

Twitch of horseflesh,
shaking off skittish adolescence.

Wishes for horses were not enough.

I herded, broke mine
to the sallow perfume of sawdust,

measuring three hundred hours
in forkloads of manure.

Sweet whiskered nicker in my palm,
my face pressed to a flank as warm as time.

I thought the ardour melted away
in a long tongue rasp over the salt lick,

but kernels falling
from a mumbled greeting set seed.

Untrampled by the staccato hoof beats
of passing time.

SOUNDS

WEI HUAN

Translated from the Chinese by Liang Yujing

I like the night,
for every sound that disappears in the day
returns.
Outside my door, someone folds his umbrella,
ascending the stairs.
The doorbell of my neighbour
occasionally rings.
The wild cries of cats scratch the windowpanes.
The freezer buzzes all the time.
I pour some herbal tea, it gurgles out
of the plastic bottle.
The clock ticks at bedside.
I bend down and feel phlegm
rolling in her throat.
Beyond the roof, stars and plants
grow in silence.
Lying on my side, I hear one of my breasts
tenderly press
against the other.

VIOLET   EOIN O'NEILL

From The Shades Of Tartarus, a collection of short tales and recollections purportedly written by the dead.

Imagine yourself attending a macabre play in a dream and becoming abstractly aware of its masked villain lurking among the audience, the performance itself serving only to distract the spectators. Such was the deep and unrelenting sense of terror which drove me through the doors of The Bloody Bacchante, only to be forcibly ejected from the establishment some hours (though they may well have been minutes) later.

I was welcomed with a thump by the frost-kissed street; another indeterminate period of time passed. The stars spun above my head, and the ringing chorus in my ears was joined by the voice of an old man.

'The cobblestones were laden with luminous specks that shimmered like distant suns,' – he spoke as if reciting some poem – 'so that it seemed as if the cosmos itself lay scattered among the shopfronts. It might almost have been a picture, if not for the objectionable presence of The Bloody Bacchante and the drunk fool who lay weeping at her feet!'

'I'm not weeping,' I informed him. 'Now piss off.'

The old man laughed. 'A poor display of aggression. Abandon it, young fellow – there is none in you! No anger, only fear and love that I can sense.'

'A poet *and* a psychic,' I muttered as he helped me to my feet.

'Fear, for many, is the cost of loving,' the old man had begun again, and though I could not see clearly, I knew that he was smiling. 'Those who love the most fear the most. Did you know that? I am much that way myself.' He laughed once more, a laugh both theatrical and sincere.

As we stumbled along together (it was becoming readily apparent that my new friend was also somewhat intoxicated) we discussed my lack of accommodation, and it was quickly agreed that the old man would provide me with 'free lodgings' on the basis that I would aid him on a certain errand. Upon my inquiry as to the specific nature of this errand the old man indulged in yet another monologue.

'You are full of love,' he said. 'You would be wise to find someone toward whom you might direct that love. Without somewhere to direct it, love becomes a burden upon the heart. This is the reason some people drink too much, why they take their own lives.'

I ignored him in the hope that he would stop speaking, but he continued: 'Violet died twelve years ago this very night. By the end she couldn't remember my name, but she could remember that she loved me ... There is an old tree that stands alone past the forest. Ancient, I should say, or beyond that – it's the oldest tree in the world, having been the only one to survive the last ice age.'

I laughed through my tears. 'What's the significance of this tree?'

'Once each year I am permitted to see her there, to enjoy her company again.'

'How lucky for you,' I said.

'When luck was being handed out on the road, I was in the field working! My father used to say that ... Since our last meeting – mine and Violet's – a fence has been erected across the safest path to the clearing. I know of no other route, and wish you to see that I climb the fence safely.'

'Would it insult you if I said that I don't believe in ghosts?' I asked him.

The old man's smile broadened further. 'Ghosts? I usually just say, people who aren't alive anymore but are paying us a little visit. But if ghosts is your preferred term ... '

'If you stare at something for long enough,' I said, 'a face usually appears.'

The old man nodded his concurrence, and for a moment I thought he would refrain from a smile.

I was surprised to find us standing at the forest's edge. It was as if the buildings had become lost among the old man's ramblings, and re-emerged as trees. 'My ears are always ringing,' he declared. 'A sound I once resolved to be that of too many thoughts clamouring at once to be heard.'

For a moment I thought to see a shape gliding above the nearby marsh. He continued as if having read my thoughts. 'To the west lies the forest. To the north, the mire, from where the shades of some antediluvian race are said to rise in winter.'

'The nights grow longer,' I muttered in my drunken contemplation.

'It bothers me more each year,' was his reply.

We entered the forest, and as we did so I was treated to a detailed account of my companion's (supposed) first encounter with his love. 'I awoke in the wood with visions of Violet,' he began, 'vivid as she was only in dreams. Her face, pallid though lovely, smiled upon me before vanishing among the vaporous gusts that surged above ... The night was black and the howl of an unseen beast echoed through the trees. My nostrils stung with the scent of scorched timber. Joining the cacophony of wind, hound and creaking oak was the shriek of a madman who burst naked from the mist. He collided with me as I laboured up sending us both crashing to the forest floor. As I lifted my face from the dirt I felt a throbbing in the back of my neck accompanied by a sensation of pressure in my eyes and ears so intense I feared they would burst. It was then I saw the sword that lay before me and I knew it was my own. I snatched the blade and rose to my feet my lungs twisting as they struggled to reclaim the wind the madman had knocked from me.'

'My first instinct was to cut him down as he frenzied but the hound was almost upon us The brute burst from the shadows growling fiercely as it rode the wind It carried limbs of smouldering ash, a tail of billowing smoke and bore no eyes I could see With a rush of valour I held my blade outward and braced to skewer the beast as it leapt but it darted past me in pursuit of the madman who had since returned to the mist. Again the forest rang with wail and roar and I would have issued a scream were it not for my throat swam with bile ...'

'As the beast gave chase to the fool I took occasion to proceed toward the glade where I knew Violet to dwell. There was her bed, which was of blue anemones floating on an emerald pond, and upon it she lay blossoming, her fair limbs flushed with desire –'

'What happened next?' I asked him.

'We made love, of course,' was his slightly indignant response.

'And the naked, shrieking madman?'

'A fellow suitor, perhaps,' said the old man as he paused beneath a break in the canopy above. 'Or something considerably darker.' He held unnaturally still in the moonlight as it poured through the break, so that I might have stood before some cadaverous sculpture. I watched as he produced a small flask from his coat pocket. He offered it to me, I drank from it, and a small fire was lit in my belly. I then offered it back to him as he stood mimicking the stance of one prepared to receive the Eucharist. The whiskey provided us with enough zeal to traverse the forest in under an hour, and as we reached the fence I thanked the stars for having spared us encounters with such monstrous beasts as the old man had depicted, saying nothing of bare-skinned lunatics (though Violet would have been a welcome sight).

I climbed the wooden fence, which was roughly six feet in height. From the top I was provided with a view of the clearing as it appeared in the small hours: a misty expanse from which rose the ancient tree. I marvelled to think that the giant oak was alive, and watched as it towered solemnly above a sea of fog set lightly aglow by the yellow moon. When I reached down to offer the old man my hand, I found that he had disappeared.

It is possible that the passing of time has embellished the images with which I associate that night, but as I trod the wet ground, trembling and cursing while the fire died inside me, I thought to see two lovers dance beneath a great oak tree.

– Unknown

Artist's Statement

Cover image: *Worn by Sanctity ... The Ambulatory At High Island* by Margaret irwin

The image comes from a monastery site of a very early settlement of hermit monks. It is on an island off the Connemara Coast called High Island, so called because of its precipitous cliffs which make access extremely difficult. There is a sort of 'chain' of such monastic remains, mostly on islands, along the west coast of Ireland. The best preserved and best known of these is that of the Skelligs.

High Island's site is probably the most recently excavated so has given some information which tells more of the daily life of the monks. There is a very complete stone-lined monastery lake fed by stone conduits down the slopes surrounding it. A stream leads out of the lake and has traces of a 'horizontal mill' for grinding whatever corn the monks grew. The chapel had been rebuilt at some time and carved burial stones were found incorporated in the walls. The 'walk-way' right round the little chapel was completely covered in grass but underneath were discovered these beautiful slabs, set in sand. They must have been an out-door cloister of sorts ... an Ambulatory. They were well used, hence my title: *Worn by Sanctity ... The Ambulatory At High Island.*

We had been taken to the island by a local fisherman friend of my husband. Over the years, my children and I have sailed out to it and I have made many visits to draw there. The access is still scary and only possible when there is no swell on the sea.

Biographical Details

Gary Allen has published fourteen collections of poetry, most recently, *Jackson's Corner*, Greenwich Exchange, London 2016. A new collection, *Mapland*, is forthcoming from Clemson University Press, South Carolina. He has been published widely in international literary magazines, including *Poetry Ireland Review*, *Irish Pages*, *The Yellow Nib*, *Ambit*, *Dark Horse*, *Fiddlehead*, *London Magazine*, *Malahat Review*, *Meanjin*, *The Poetry Review*, *Prairie Schooner*, *Stand*, *The Threepenny Review*, etc.

Simon Anton Diego Baena's work has been published in *The Bitter Oleander*, *Catamaran Literary Reader*, *Rust+Moth*, *Gravel*, *Glass: A Journal of Poetry*, *UCity Review*, *Osiris*, *The James Franco Review* and others.

Joe Carrick-Varty is a writer based in Manchester. He studied English Literature with Creative Writing.

Emily Cullen is a Galway-based poet, scholar and harper. She is the author of two collections of poetry: *In Between Angels and Animals* (Arlen House, 2013) and *No Vague Utopia* (Ainnir Publishing, 2003). She was selected for Poetry Ireland's Introductions Series in 2004. She has performed internationally with a variety of music ensembles and recorded on a number of albums. In addition to her creative writing, she publishes articles on Irish cultural history and teaches part-time at NUI Galway.

Barbara De Franceschi is an Australian poet. Her work has been published widely in Australia, in other countries and online. In 2015 she was the artist-in-residence for the University Department of Rural Health in the remote outback city of Broken Hill as part of the *Art in Health* programme. She is currently a committee member of the *Arts in Wellbeing* initiative for the Far West Local Health District and shares her creative writing skills with nursing home residents and the community at large.

Kate Dempsey's poetry is published in many journals in Ireland and the UK. Prizes include The Plough Prize and Hennessy New Irish Writing Award (shortlisted). Her debut collection, *The Space Between,* was published by Doire Press in 2016 from which she had a poem selected as highly commended for the Forward Prize.

Maurice Devitt was selected for the Poetry Ireland Introductions Series and shortlisted for the Listowel Poetry Collection Competition in 2016. Winner of the Trócaire/Poetry Ireland Competition in 2015, he has been placed or shortlisted in many competitions including the Patrick Kavanagh Award, Over the Edge New Writer Competition, Cúirt New Writing Award, Cork Literary Review and the Doire Press International Chapbook Competition. A guest poet at the Poets in Transylvania festival in 2015, he has had poems published in various journals in Ireland, England, Scotland, the US, Mexico, Romania, India and Australia. He is curator of the Irish Centre for Poetry Studies site and a founder member of the Hibernian Writers' Group.

Liz Dolan's poetry manuscript, *A Secret of Long Life,* nominated for a Pushcart, was published by Cave Moon Press. Her first poetry collection, *They Abide,* nominated for The McGovern Prize, Ashland University was published by March Street.

Brenda Donoghue is originally from Beara in Co. Kerry. She now lives in Co. Cork with her family.

Honor Duff's poetry has been published previously in *Crannóg*, *The Stony Thursday Book*, *Skylight 47*, *Boyne Berries* and *Windows Art & Artists*. She was shortlisted for the Red Line Poetry Awards, Dublin, in 2016.

Kate Ennals is a poet and short story writer. Her first poetry collection, *AT The Edge*, came out in September 2015, published by Lapwing. She is regularly published in various literary publications such as *Crannóg*, *Skylight 47*, *Burning Bush 2*, *The Galway Review*, *Ropes*, *Boyne Berries*, *North West Words*, *New Ulster Anthology*, *The International Lakeview Journal* and featured in *The Spark*. Her work was shortlisted (and performed) at the Claremorris Fringe festival, the Swift Festival, in the Doolin Short Story competition, 2014, and the Stephen King short story competition, 2015.

Jarlath Fahy joined the Focus Theatre Group in 1984 where he studied the Stanislavski Method of Acting under Deirdre O'Connor. From acting and directing with Focus he relocated to Berlin where he joined the Berlin English Language Theatre. On his return to Ireland he joined the Gung Ho Theatre Company at The King's Head, Galway staging *Lone Star*, and acted with the Taboo Theatre Company, touring with Willy Russell's *Stags and Hens*. As a student in NUIG his poetry appeared in *Criterion*, the Arts Society Magazine, and in *Outlet*, the journal of the Philosophical Society. He completed a poetry masterclass with Ian Duhig and his poetry has since been published in *Crannóg* magazine, *WOW!* and in the collection *during which nothing happens* – the Writers Writing Live event of Galway's Project '06 Festival. His first collection is *The Man Who Was Haunted By Beautiful Smells* (Wordsonthestreet, 2007).

Michael Farry was selected for Poetry Ireland Introductions in 2011. His first poetry collection, *Asking for Directions*, was published by Doghouse Books, Tralee, in 2012. His poetry has been published in journals and anthologies in Ireland, the UK, America, Israel, Australia and Canada. His history book, *Sligo, The Irish Revolution 1912-1923*, was published in 2012 by Four Courts Press, Dublin.

Agnieszka Filipek is in the process of translating her poetry into English. In September 2016 she was awarded a distinction in the poetry competition Polowy and took part in the three day Underground Education Workshops held by Biuro Literackie during the Station Literature 21 Festival in Stronie Śląskie in Poland.

Anton Floyd was born in Egypt and now lives in Inchigeeagh, West Cork. His poems have been published in *The Stony Thursday Book*, *Ghent Review*, *Live Encounters* and *Shamrock Haiku*. He won the International Haiku Competition of the Irish Haiku Society (2014), got honourable mention (2015) and was runner up in the Snapshot Press (UK) Haiku Calendar (2016). He is a member of the Irish Haiku Society. A selection of his haiku was published in *Between the Leaves* ed. Anatoly Kudryavitsky (Arlen House, 2016), an anthology of new haiku writing from Ireland.

Shauna Gilligan writes short and long stories and is interested in the depiction of historical events in fiction, and creative processes. Her stories have been published in journals such as *The Stinging Fly* and *Gargoyle*. She is currently working on her second novel set in Mexico.

Wei Huan, penname of Cui Yuwei, was born in 1983 and is a Chinese poet based in Zhuhai, where she works as a university lecturer. She became known among the Chinese poetry circle for her confessional, provocative way of writing about her personal life.

Margaret Irwin was born in India of Irish parents and grew up in Co. Wicklow. After taking her primary degree in languages at Trinity College, Dublin, she chose to train as a painter at the studio of the cubist teacher Andre Lhote in Paris. She has exhibited in many juried and open shows both in England and Ireland and has received various awards and residencies. Her work is held by a number of public bodies as well as by private collectors. In 2008 she received a Lifetime Achievement Award from Galway County Council. She now works in her chosen medium of etching, as well as painting, in her studio at Claddaghduff in north Connemara, Ireland. She continues to exhibit and holds periodic printmaking workshops in the Adult Education facility at Letterfrack Co. Galway. Her imagery is mostly figurative and drawn from observation. Much of it refers to the Early Christian and Prehistoric sites which abound in the area. She says: 'From my figurative images I seek to draw out greater resonances that suggest their cultural and social contexts.' margaretirwinwest@gmail.com   www.margaretirwinwest.com.

Ríona Judge McCormack works in international development. She is the 2016 Hennessy New Irish Writer of the Year and winner of the inaugural Galley Beggar Press Short Story Prize. She lives in Johannesburg, where she is editing her first novel.

Patrick Kehoe's first poems were published by the late James Liddy in Gorey Arts Centre broadsheets and issues of *The Gorey Detail*. Early poems appeared in the *Irish Press* and *St Stephens* (UCD). In recent times, his work has been heard on RTÉ Radio 1's *Sunday Miscellany* and on RTÉ Lyric FM, while poems have appeared in *Cyphers*, *The Irish Times*, *The Stony Thursday Book*, *Enniscorthy Echo*, *Natural Bridge*, *The Scaldy Detail*, *Red Lamp Black Piano* and *Dust Motes Dancing in the Sunbeams*. His debut collection, *It's Words You Want*, was published by Salmon Poetry in July 2011. *The Cask of Moonlight* was published by Dedalus Press, September 2014.

Shannon Kelly's work has appeared in journals and at conferences throughout the United States, and she is the 2016 winner of the Allingham Festival Poetry Competition.

Brian Kirk was shortlisted twice for the Hennessy New Irish Writing Awards for fiction. His first poetry collection *After The Fall* is published by Salmon Poetry, 2017. His novel for children *The Rising Son* was published in December 2015. He is a member of the Hibernian Writers Workshop and he blogs at www.briankirkwriter.com.

Rozz Lewis was highly commended for the Over the Edge New Writer of the Year 2016. Her stories have been published in the anthology *What Champagne Was Like*, and literary magazines such as *Boyne Berries*, *Wordlegs*, *Silver Apples*, *Spontaneity*, *Galway Review*, *Bray Arts Journal* and *Literary Orphans*.

James Martyn Joyce is from Galway where he is a member of The Talking Stick Workshop. His first collection of poetry, *Shedding Skin*, was published by Arlen House in 2010. His collection of short stories, *What's Not Said*, followed in 2012. He contributed a story to and edited the dark fiction collection, *Noir by Noir West*, in 2014.

Mary Melvin Geoghegan has four collections of poetry published. Her latest is *Say it Like a Paragraph* with Bradshaw Books, Cork (2012). Her next collection *As Moon and Mother Collide* will be published with Salmon Poetry in 2017. Her work has been widely published, including *Poetry Ireland Review*, *Crannóg*, *Skylight*, *THE SHOp*, *Cyphers*, *Studies*, *The Sunday Times*, *The Moth*, *Boyne Berries*, *The Stony Thursday Book*, *Oxfam Calendar*, *Siarsceal Anthology* amongst others. She has edited several anthologies of children's poetry and is a member of the Edgeworth Literary Society.

Geraldine Mills is the author of three collections of short stories and four collections of poetry for adults. She has been awarded many prizes and bursaries including the Hennessy/Tribune New Irish Writer Award, two Arts Council Bursaries and a Patrick and Katherine Kavanagh Fellowship. She is a mentor with NUI Galway and an online tutor with Creative Writing Ink. Her first children's novel titled *Gold* has just been published by Little Island.

Lisa Morris is a freeverse and formalist poet, nature explorer, artist and traveller. Formerly an agent for authors, she is now author of two books, *Your Love is Inconvenient and Sublime* available on Kindle, and *The Sorcerer and Other Poems* available through Rainfall Books.

Elizabeth Morton is a New Zealand writer. She has been published in *Poetry NZ*, *PRISM international*, *Cordite*, *JAAM*, *Shot Glass Journal*, *Takahe Magazine*, *Blackmail Press*, *Meniscus*, *Flash Frontier*, *SmokeLong Quarterly*, *the Sunday Star Times*, *Literary Orphans*, and *Island Magazine* among others. Her prose is in *The Best Small Fictions 2016*.

Mark Mullee currently lives and works in Rotterdam, the Netherlands. His poems have appeared previously in *Crannóg*, as well as other publications in Ireland and the US – most recently in *Untameable City*, an anthology about his native city, Houston, Texas.

Mark O'Flynn is an Australian novelist and poet who has been widely published. His fifth collection of poems was published in 2015. His latest book is the novel *The Last Days of Ava Langdon*, 2016.

Eoin O'Neill is a professional videographer and sound technician based in Dublin. He writes short fiction, often with musical accompaniment.

Christine Pacyk is a poet and educator from Chicago. She holds an MFA in poetry from Northwestern University. Her work has been published in *Monsters and Dust*, *Jet Fuel Review*, *Canopic Jar*, *Beloit Poetry Journal*, and is forthcoming in *Kettle Blue Review*.

Diana Powell is a winner of a PENfro short story competition. This year, she was a runner-up in the Cinnamon Prize, longlisted for the Sean O'Faoláin Award, and shortlisted for the Over the Edge New Writer Prize. She has been published in *The Lonely Crowd*, *Brittle Star*, *Dream Catcher* and *The Next Review*. Her Cinnamon story will feature in an anthology next year.

Shannon Quinn is the author of the poetry collection, *Questions for Wolf* (Thistledown Press). Her work has appeared in literary journals in Canada, the US and the UK.

John Reinhart lives on a farmlette in Dust Bowl, USA. He is a Frequent Contributor at the Songs of Eretz, member of the Science Fiction Poetry Association, and was awarded the 2016 Horror Writers Association Dark Poetry Scholarship. His chapbook, *encircled*, is available from Prolific Press. More of his work is available at http://www.patreon.com/johnreinhart

Clare Sawtell lives near Kinvara, Co. Galway. She has been published in *Crannóg*, *THE SHOp*, *The Stony Thursday Book* and *Earthlines*. Her poetry collection, *The Next Dance*, was published by Wordsonthestreet in 2014.

Jonathan Starke is founding editor of *Palooka* and has published essays and stories in *The Sun*, *Missouri Review*, *Threepenny Review*, *Greensboro Review*, *North American Review* and others.

Chelsea Steinauer-Scudder grew up between the Midwest and New England. She holds a Master of Theological Studies from Harvard Divinity School and is currently working on her first book, a work of narrative non-fiction featuring a series of stories about the human relationship to place, land, and home, collected during a pilgrimage.

Gerry Stewart is a poet, editor and creative writing tutor currently living in Finland with her family. Her poetry collection, *Post-Holiday Blues*, was published by Flambard Press.

Karina Tynan was highly commended in the Patrick Kavanagh Poetry Award in 2015. She has previously had poetry published in *THE SHOp* and *Crannóg*. She was shortlisted for the Wow poetry award and subsequently published in the *Wow anthology* in 2011. She has also had one memoir published in *The Little Book Of Christmas Memories* published by Liberties Press in 2013.

Karla Van Vliet is the author of *From the Book of Remembrance* (Shanti Arts, 2015), a collection of poems and paintings, and *The River From My Mouth* (Shanti Arts, 2016), a full-length collection of poems. She has been a featured author on the Blue Heron Speaks page of BHR and nominated for a Pushcart Prize. Her poems have appeared in such journals as *Poet Lore, Blue Heron Review, The Tishman Review, Green Mountains Review, Found Poetry Review* and *Painted Bride Quarterly*. She holds an MFA in poetry from Vermont College of Fine Arts and is a co-founder and editor of *deLuge Journal*, a literary and arts journal.

Anne Walsh Donnelly's stories have been published online, in print and broadcast on RTÉ Radio 1. She has been shortlisted in several competitions including the Over the Edge New Writer of the Year Award (2014 and 2016), the Fish International Short Story Prize (2015) and the RTÉ Radio 1 Francis MacManus Short Story Competition (2014 and 2015).

Máiríde Woods writes poetry and short stories. Her work has appeared in anthologies and reviews and on RTÉ radio. She has won several prizes including two Hennessy awards, the Francis MacManus and a PJ O'Connor award. Two collections of her poetry, *The Lost Roundness of the World* and *Unobserved Moments of Change*, have been published by Astrolabe. One of her poems appears in the recent anthology, *If Ever You Go to Dublin Town*.

Liang Yujing is a bilingual poet and translator currently based in Wellington, New Zealand. His poems and translations have appeared in a number of magazines across the world, recently in *Modern Poetry in Translation, Acumen* and *Boston Review*. He is also the Chinese translator of *Best New Zealand Poems 2014*.

Stay in touch with Crannóg
@
www.crannogmagazine.com

Lightning Source UK Ltd.
Milton Keynes UK
UKOW01f0324170217
294636UK00002B/34/P